Highland Fling

Highland Fling

Kathleen Ernst

Cricket Books
Chicago

Grateful acknowledgment is given to the following for permission to reprint the copyrighted material below:

Duart Music, London, for excerpted lyrics from "Ballad of Glen Coe," words and music by Jim McLean, copyright © 1963 by Duart Music, London, UK.

Library of Congress Cataloging-in-Publication Data

Ernst, Kathleen.
    Highland fling / Kathleen Ernst.—1st ed.
      p. cm.
    Summary: Having moved to North Carolina with her mother and sister following her parents' divorce, fifteen-year-old Tanya tries to ignore her anger at her family while also making some unexpected connections with her Scottish heritage.
    ISBN-13: 978-0-8126-2742-8
    ISBN-10: 0-8126-2742-3
 [1. Anger—Fiction. 2. Scottish Americans—Fiction. 3. Divorce—Fiction. 4. Identity—Fiction. 5. North Carolina —Fiction.] I. Title.
    PZ7.E7315Hig 2006
    [Fic]—dc22

2005030284

For Meghan—
Thanks for choosing such a cool school.

Chapter 1

A crush of girls in kilts and velvet vests or jackets mobbed the corridors outside the auditorium. I clawed my way into the ladies' room so I could check my own regulation attire. The porcelain sink felt cool beneath my sweating palms as I stared at my reflection. I'd told my mom I didn't mind having a "preowned" kilt, and from the handful of choices I'd chosen a purply blue-on-cream plaid, with a touch of green, that reminded me of lupines blooming along the shore of Lake Superior. Now, as best I could tell, I'd met the guidelines established by the Scottish Official Board of Highland Dancing. The lacy-sleeved blouse peeking from my vest was dazzlingly white. My competitor's number was pinned square onto my skirt. I'd varnished my hair into a severe bun.

"Does *anyone* have any nail polish remover?"

"Do you think the judges will care if I wear tiny posts? I just got my ears pierced, and I have to wear *something*."

"Don't tell me my hair looks good! You'll *jinx* me!"

Chatter bounced off the tile floor to ricochet in my brain. The curling iron a dancer was using on her bangs added a scorched layer to the muggy air. A girl behind me, hopping on one foot as she pulled on a plaid knee-sock, almost knocked me into the sink. I was surrounded by high-strung escapees from that old movie *Brigadoon.*

What was I doing here? Why had I let myself get talked into competing? I swallowed hard, turned away from the mirror, and crouched to scrabble in my big dance bag. My camcorder, wrapped in a towel, rested beneath my ordinary clothes. I felt my blood pressure ease back toward normal as my Panasonic nestled against my palm, familiar as an old friend. It's not the newest model, but this little baby still boasts an optical zoom lens, manual focus ring for artistic tinkering, and crystal-clear image. Sweet.

I flipped out the LCD monitor, switched the automatic–exposure mode to low light, and began capturing the dancers' preparations for the first local competition of the year. I caught the look of concentration on a pudgy eight-year-old's face as she laced the dancing shoes called ghillies onto her feet. I caught a girl about ten years older applying blush and then blotting it off, trying for that you-can't-tell-I'm-wearing-makeup look. I caught a frazzled mom sewing a button onto a moss-green velvet vest while her daughter jiggled anxiously beside her. Then, camera still whirring companionably, I slid into the hall.

This Saturday competition was being held at my own high school, but since I'd rather lie down in traffic than join the drama club, I'd never been backstage before. Two nervously giggling girls shoved past, popping jellybeans. A cherry-cheeked girl sat on the floor, rubbing a tiny stuffed dog swathed in yellow-red-black plaid—for luck, I guess. Beginners self-consciously practiced their steps. Seasoned competitors practiced their steps with carefully choreographed nonchalance, or jumped up and down to loosen their muscles while leaning on a friend's shoulder for balance. This was good stuff. I might need these shots one day.

I focused on a purple-kilted cutie with closed eyes who was muttering to herself as she visualized her dance steps. She couldn't be more than six and was, therefore, one of the lucky munchkins in the Primary level. They would open the day's competition, and no matter how off-step they became as they hopped back and forth on stage, the audience would smile adoringly and applaud like mad. Oh, to be young and limber and cute.

Any documentary gains audience appeal with the inclusion of a sweet little kid, so I spent extra tape on this one. I was backing around a corner, easing into a wide shot, when—*blam!* I collided with another girl. I whirled in time to see her stumble into the man behind her. He already had one hand on her shoulder, and he grabbed her elbow with his other hand to steady her.

"Oh! Thanks, Dad," she exclaimed, and then to me, "I'm so sorry!"

I had never seen her before. She was maybe fifteen like me, maybe a year older. Her red velvet jacket fit so well I knew it had been tailored for her, not bought secondhand from her dance teacher's closet. She had a round face and hair the color of dried mud and an amazing smile.

My hands clenched the camcorder so hard it hurt. A flash of hot anger made me take another step backwards.

What was *that* all about? Get a grip, Zeshonski! I ordered myself. Geez! I'd escaped with only a whack in the elbow from her dance bag, and since I'd been the one walking backwards, I could hardly blame her.

The girl's smile faded. "Are you O.K.?"

Somewhere behind me a dancer shrieked, "Mom, I need another *safety pin!*" I opened my mouth. Closed it. Shook my head.

"Why don't I head out to the auditorium and find your mother, Sunshine," the girl's dad said. A full salt-and-pepper beard balanced his receding hairline. He had the same come-from-the-inside smile as his daughter, and the corners of his eyes had a crinkled look—as if he used that smile a lot. "Highland fling first up today?"

"Nope, the sword dance."

"Well, good luck." He hitched up the big camera bag hanging from his shoulder.

The girl fixed him with A Look. "Just don't embarrass me this time, O.K.?"

"No promises." He squeezed her shoulder, nodded at me, and disappeared around the corner.

The girl smiled after him, then turned back to me. "You know what?" she asked, her face going soft with sympathy. "I bet you just have a case of nerves. I was a wreck at my first competition. This is your first, right? I don't remember seeing you before."

"Um, y-yes," I managed. Like a complete dork.

"You'll do fine." She flashed that smile again. It wasn't fakey at all, and it lit up her whole face. "My name is Christina, by the way. Good luck!" Then she walked on by.

I leaned against the wall, rubbing my arms. The air conditioning, so lacking in the bathroom, was evidently set at "Popsicle" in this back hall. My chest felt tight. I was clearly losing it. I couldn't remember ever feeling like this. Did this stupid dance thing really have me that torqued up?

Fortunately, whatever assailed me drained away as quickly as it had come. Once Christina disappeared, I no longer felt like death warmed on toast. I shuddered like a wet dog, ridding myself of the last bad vibes. Weird. Very weird.

I considered my camcorder with longing, but was uncomfortably aware of time ticking toward the witching hour. Emphasizing the point, one of the coordinator ladies walked down the hall calling, "Primary dancers to the staging area, please. Beginners, be ready." That was me: Big-time Beginner. Time to step in front of the camera.

Once the tiny Primary dancers had been herded toward the stage, I made my way back to the bathroom, eyeing my competitors as I went. Some looked no older than seven. Was I the oldest Beginner in the whole friggin' competition? Miss Janet, of the Flora MacDonald School of Highland Dance, had assured me that would not be the case.

Apparently Miss Janet was wrong. An official hurried by with an armful of ceremonial swords, and I considered snatching one and putting it to a use definitely not sanctioned by the Scottish Official Board of Highland Dancing.

Back in the ladies' room, as I locked my camcorder in my bag, a familiar voice squealed into my ear. "Oh, Tanya, isn't this exciting?"

"A thrill a minute," I told my sister. Nan was twelve and thought all this Scottish stuff was just swell. Nan was born Nancy, but when we moved back to the North Carolina homeplace a year ago, she plunged into denial like Mom and decided to "reclaim her Scottish heritage" in a big way. She wanted to be called Nanag, which is pronounced "NAN-ak" and means "Wee Nancy" in Gaelic. Nan was the absolute best I could muster.

"Let me see you." I stood back and surveyed her attire. After talking Mom into having a new kilt made, Nan had of course chosen the MacDonald dress tartan, which features generous stripes of red, blue, green, black, and white. MacDonald is my middle name, and our mother's birth name.

"Suspenders feel O.K.?" I asked. She nodded eagerly. "Garters not too tight?" She nodded again. Petite Nan needed the power of hidden elastic to keep her kilt and socks from sliding to the floor when she started hopping about on stage.

I twisted her around so I could check her bun. I was worried that her fine hair might escape the net holding it in place. "I think you need some extra hairpins—"

"Extra hairpins?" She instantly panicked. "I don't have any!"

"I packed them for you." Nan is not a well-organized person, and I was used to thinking for both of us. In this case a plastic travel bag with see-through pockets designated for hair supplies, makeup, sewing stuff, etc., made final adjustments easy. It only took me a few seconds to secure the wisps that had threatened to slip free. "There," I said, nodding. "Now you look perfect."

Nan flexed and pointed one foot, then the other. "Do you think I'll do O.K.?"

"Touch the very tips of your toes on the pointing steps," I reminded her. "And don't let your arms wilt."

"I won't," she promised breathlessly, then darted away

with a tardy "Thanks!" tossed over her shoulder. We were both competing in the sword dance, but her round would come before mine because she was younger.

As expected, the audience's approval for the tiny tots in Primary echoed backstage. Then the sound system emitted an ear-shattering screech and crackle as the first three Beginner dancers were announced. I took a sip from my water bottle and sprinkled a few drops on the soles of my ghillies to reduce the chance of slipping. I heard the bagpiper accompanying the competition begin the only tune used for the sword dance, *"Gillie Chalium."* That translates into something like "Columba, servant of God." Miss Janet says this association with Saint Columba represents the symbolic victory of good over evil.

I could use a victory, symbolic or otherwise. The shrill tones made my muscles tighten. I saw Christina and some other girls with the look of top-level dancers—Premier class—playing a relaxed game of Go Fish on the floor. All around me other Beginner dancers were leaping and flinging. I probably should have done some leaping and flinging myself, to warm up. But I didn't.

When an official called Nan's number, I watched her disappear into the murky light of stage right and sent a plea to the Highland gods: *Please let her do O.K. Please, just let her do O.K.* Nan reappeared after her round, flushed and breathless and beaming. I gave her a thumbs-up. She held crossed fingers high, then pointed at me. I accepted her good luck with a tiny smile. Maybe I'd actually get through this.

When my number was called fifteen minutes later, I reported to the official clipboard-toting woman in the wings. She lined three of us up for the next round. "Don't go out yet," she ordered, as if we might bolt onto the stage and elbow aside the three girls already hopping about in the sword dance. I rubbed my palms on my kilt.

The music stopped, the audience applauded, and the three sweaty dancers marched primly offstage, smiles glued in place. "Miriam McPherson, Tanya Zeshonski, Tiffany Blue!" the clipboard woman hissed frantically. "Go, go!"

Highland dancers are trained to turn out from the hips down, and the three of us duck-walked to our places. I was in the center, with a short brunette on one side and an even shorter redhead on the other. We each stepped into place before a pair of Highland broadswords positioned on the stage in front of us so they crossed at right angles. Miss Janet's voice rang in my head: "Back straight! Head up! Knees out!"

I could just make out the judges' table beyond the lights. Hold it together, I told myself. You *can* do this. You *can* get on a stage without disaster. Then the piper, surely bored out of his mind by now, started another round of *"Gillie Chalium."* We bowed and began to dance.

The sword dance, say those who know such things, was first performed by Highland warriors on the eve of battle. At one time only men danced the sword dance, but the choreography remained the same when women began to compete. It involves hopping daintily about the crossed swords in an intricate series of steps. A dancer must never touch one of the swords with her foot.

I kicked one of mine—oh, say fifteen seconds into the dance.

If a Highland warrior kicked one of *his* swords, he knew he would fall in battle.

If a Highland dancer kicks one of *her* swords—at least as hard as I kicked mine—she must stop dancing and stand at attention while the other competitors continue.

I stepped back, the metallic clang of that kicked sword still ringing in my ears. I willed myself not to throw up the lentil burger I'd snarfed an hour earlier. The ancient Highland warriors, doomed to a painful and bloody death, could not have felt worse for kicking the cursed sword than I did. If I was producing a documentary about this event, I'd whisper in the videographer's ear to pull in for a tight shot of the screwup dancer's face.

A sword dance lasts about five minutes. I used that eternity to make a mental list of all the people responsible for this disaster:

My father, for walking out on Mom over a year ago.

My mother, for selling our Wisconsin house and hauling our Northern butts down to our "ancestral home" in North Carolina.

Nan, who talked me into taking dance lessons "for Mom's sake."

And me, for being stupid enough to let Nan do that.

The brunette and the redhead clapped their hands, signaling the piper to speed up to quick time. Sweat dribbled down my forehead. I wasn't allowed to wipe it off. I hated that feeling. I hated Highland dancing. I hated the sword dance in particular. The blaring drone and wail went on and on and *on*. Perhaps the piper had lost his place and started over. Why did they let an inexperienced piper play for competition, anyway?

The bagpipes' wail was unendurable. These were no little uilleann pipes, but the wicked big ones. The ones used to lead those ancient Highland warriors into battle. The ones the British once banned as weapons of war. The ones that send icy shivers down the spine and curdle the blood.

Bagpipes. Those I hated most of all.

Chapter 2

When the bagpiper finally ran out of breath, I walked woodenly offstage with the other two girls. Then I bolted. On my way to the ladies' room I knocked a girl doing a sprightly Highland fling into the wall, and I didn't look back. I wanted to hide in a stall, but the bathroom was so crowded all I could do was snatch my dance bag and change in front of the sinks, hopping from one foot to the other.

I was moving at the speed of light, and almost disguised in jeans and a Lake Superior T-shirt, before Nan caught up with me. One look at her face, and I knew she'd been watching. "Oh, *Tanya*," she breathed mournfully.

"Nan, just shut—up." I tried to stuff my kilt into the dance bag. It did not *want* to be stuffed into the dance bag. I scooped up the whole mess and fled.

"But, Tanya!" she wailed. "You've still got the reel!" Her voice faded as she tried unsuccessfully to eel through the dancers in my wake. "And the Highland fli-i-i-ing!"

I ran down the hall and emerged into the lobby in front of the auditorium. And there was Mom. I couldn't figure out if I was sorry or glad to see her.

"Hi, sweetie," she said.

I could hear the bagpipes' screech through the closed doors. I ungritted my teeth long enough to say hi back.

She regarded me. Mom has brown hair she usually pulls back in a barrette, and a faint smattering of freckles on her cheeks. The combination makes her look younger than she really is. Her dark eyes are different, though. They are old-person wise. One look in those eyes just then, and I could tell what she was thinking. I shook my head. I did *not* want to talk about it.

"Shall I take you home?" she asked finally.

Yes! I wanted to shout. Home to Wisconsin!

But I couldn't say that to my mom. After what my dad had put her through, she didn't need me giving her grief. So I took a deep breath and shook my head. "No. We'd miss one of Nan's rounds if we did that. I'll come sit with you." I was rewarded when the tight look on Mom's face eased a smidge.

I braced myself as we slid back into the darkened auditorium. And for the next three and a half hours, I sat on a miserably hard seat and clapped on cue. I did notice, with a sense of vindication, that an obviously newbie piper was on the scene. The head piper was a gray-haired man, big and square, who seemed to know what he was doing. The younger guy, maybe my age, occasionally played a piece by himself. I was sure that skinny kid had played for my round.

Ultimately Christina, the girl I'd bumped into earlier, won four medals. Christina Campbell, from the Misty Glen School of Highland Dance. Her father stood up a few rows in front of me and bellowed, "Way to go, Christina!" and snapped some photos. I wondered how it felt to make your dad proud like that.

Several of the more experienced dancers from the Flora MacDonald School of Highland Dance were awarded medals, so I figured Miss Janet would go home happy. Nan didn't win anything, but she had danced well for her first competition, so I figured she and Mom would go home happy, too.

"And now for our most coveted award," the announcer said, ignoring the microphone's squeal. It was practically indistinguishable from a bagpipe, so she probably didn't notice. "Our Premier champion today is . . . Christina Campbell!"

More squeals, more applause, more bellows from the proud papa. Christina stepped forward with perfectly pointed feet. She bowed and thanked the judge calmly, but after accepting her trophy, she glanced toward her parents and let loose that amazing smile. She didn't look too embarrassed. My fingers curled into fists.

"She's a lovely girl," Mom said, then glanced at me. "Tanya? Are you O.K.?"

"Sure, Mom," I managed. "Sure."

Mom was considerate enough not to drag me backstage to look for Nan. While we waited in the lobby, the two pipers walked by. Close up, the young guy looked unlikely in his kilt. His skin was a lovely shade of olive; his eyes and hair dark. As they passed, he happened to glance my way, and his eyes widened. No doubt he was surprised to see me, the screwup, still hanging around.

"Have we met?" he asked, a frown appearing between his brows.

I realized my face had settled into a scowl. "No," I said shortly, then felt my cheeks flush. "Um, sorry." I gave my best impression of a smile. He shrugged and turned back to his companion, and they walked away with their instruments over their shoulders. I watched the red tassels that hung from the big pipes swing back and forth until the two pipers disappeared. I had a headache.

"*Mom!*" The squeal was unmistakably Nan. She ran to join us, lugging her dance bag. "Did you see me? Did you see?"

Mom kissed Nan's forehead. "I did see, honey. We both did. You were marvelous. I'm so proud." Mom's gaze darted to me, as if gauging how much of this I could handle. I felt sorry for her, because this was about as awkward as it could be: one dancer, one disaster, and one mom.

"You did good, you little runt," I said.

Nan beamed, then suddenly stopped short. "Oh-h-h,"

she breathed, and offered Christina Campbell, who was walking past with her parents, a tentative smile. "You danced *be-yoo-tifully.*"

Christina paused and smiled. "Thank you. And you did a nice job, too. I noticed especially during the Highland fling."

Nan turned to Mom, too ecstatic for words. Then Christina looked at me and put a hand on my arm. It was fish-belly white. "Don't mind," she said softly. "Try practicing with the swords set on tuna fish cans. You'll get used to raising your feet."

While standing rocklike on stage, I hadn't imagined that *anything* could make me feel worse than I already did. I had been wrong.

"Are you two sisters?" Christina asked.

Nan made breathless introductions and told Christina the Wondergirl where we studied dance.

"There's going to be a dance clinic this Wednesday in Fayetteville. Did you hear about it?" Christina smiled. "It's a chance for us to get the kinks out before the summer Games really get rolling."

I'd almost forgotten I was facing a summer of Highland Games. Oh, joy.

"You should come," Christina urged, including us both in the invitation. "It'll be a lot of fun, and I'd be glad to give you some pointers if you like."

"I'm driving, if you need a ride," added her mom, a

short, round woman who looked genetically incapable of producing such a leggy child.

"That would be great!" Nan gasped joyfully.

"I—don't—think—so," I said at the same time. My voice came out much louder than I'd intended, and colder as well. Everybody stared at me. The smile faded from Christina's face. Her parents exchanged frowns.

My cheeks burned again. What was the *matter* with me? "I think I'll wait in the car," I announced, and fled.

I didn't have much to say on the ride home, or during dinner. I'm sure Mom thought I was devastated about the whole sword-kicking thing, but that wasn't it. Well, not entirely, anyway.

I couldn't stop thinking about Christina Campbell. I had not exactly done a whiz-bang job of making new friends here in North Carolina. When I started school, no one noticed me for three weeks. One day a hair-netted lunch lady had asked something in her unintelligible drawl. "Um, clam chowder over *biscuits?*" I asked. Suddenly things got real quiet. Then the jock in line behind me burst out laughing. "It's *gravy,* moron," he'd cackled.

Moron. Moron. Moron. For a moment that echo drowned the memory of those cursed bagpipes, and I hated North Carolina so badly I tasted it, sour on my tongue. I'd been dragged to a place where people put gravy on their biscuits and sugar in their tea and bacon bits in *everything.*

Still, I could not remember ever taking such an intense, immediate dislike to someone. It wasn't jealousy. I didn't like Christina before I even knew she was a prima flinger. Christina had obviously moved through Beginner, Novice, and Intermediate levels while I was still building snowmen in Green Bay. But by all rights, she should also be pencil-thin and beautiful and snooty. The cheerleader type. Now *that's* a girl you can hate without regret. Christina was definitely not beautiful. Even worse than that: Christina was friendly. She did not act stuck-up.

I hoped I never saw her again.

Chapter 3

*F*ilmmaking is complex. Make a documentary without heart, and you'll be left holding something flat and lifeless. Ignore artistry, and you don't do justice to the medium. And without mastering the technical skills of videography, sound, and editing, you'll sink deep in doo the first time you try to get decent backlight on a cloudy day, or interview a soft-spoken child, or enhance a shot in postproduction.

Independent filmmaking is most challenging of all, but I knew already that my road did not lead to a commercial station—or even PBS. At big stations everything is divvied up amongst engineers and lighting directors and recordists and graphic designers. Not to mention producers. Even at little old WPNE in Green Bay, I'd met executive producers and series producers and plain old producers, and associate producers and assistant producers. But indies travel light—at least at the beginning of their careers—and they alone are responsible for transforming their vision into finished product. Indies schlep their own light boxes and cables, recharge their own batteries, edit their own scripts, make their own phone calls, arrange their own logistics for field shoots. The reward? Total control.

I've always known I was up to it. Heart? Passion drips from my projects. Artistry? I never settle for a straight shot when I can pan; never shoot at noon if I can wait for late day's soft golden light. My technical skills need developing, but I'm working on that. And I have an uncanny sense of organization. I am comfortable saying, with complete modesty, that I was born to make documentaries.

Unfortunately, I was not yet in film school, and my heart, artistry, and technical ability—much less my supreme organizational skills—were all too often unappreciated. I knew I was in trouble when Mrs. Martingale asked me to stay after Contemporary Issues class on Monday afternoon.

While everyone else raced for the door, I shuffled to her desk. "Tanya," she said, waving some papers in the air. "What is this?" She shook her head, and her big red parrot earrings danced over her shoulders in bizarre contrast to her tone. Mrs. Martingale wore some kind of bird earrings nine days out of ten.

"My final project," I mumbled. Kids in the hall shouted and slammed locker doors. The last period of the day was over, and everyone else had better things to do.

"What was the assignment?"

I felt my cheeks get warm. "Well . . . we were supposed to investigate a current political issue and write it up."

"Write an *essay*, Tanya. My instructions were clear. What is this?"

"It's . . . it's a treatment for a documentary about the clashes between environmentalists and the fishing industry in the Caribbean." I didn't know whether to feel upset or self-righteous. I'd gotten so excited about everything I'd found while doing research that it hadn't occurred to me that Mrs. Martingale would care whether I presented my findings in pure essay form or not.

Mrs. Martingale tapped her pen against the offensive pages. "This is not the assignment."

"But it's good work!" It *was*. I'd summarized the problem and outlined the flow of a documentary. I'd even included a script and list of proposed visuals, properly presented in columns.

"I can't accept this, Tanya. You did not follow instructions." She laid the paper on the desk. I saw a red F penciled in the margin.

An *F*? "But—but I covered all the specific points you asked for," I stammered. "It's extremely well organized. I cited sources, and presented both sides of the issue, and—"

"And you did not follow instructions." Mrs. Martingale's eyes, magnified behind oversized glasses, were unyielding.

How could a woman who wore red parrot earrings be so inflexible? Couldn't I be rewarded for creativity? For individual thought?

Apparently not. I didn't waste any more time in argument, just grabbed the paper and walked out. In the hall, I took a deep breath, mentally figuring the impact of that stupid F on my final grade. I'd be lucky to get a C this quarter.

I sighed, flattening my spine against the bank of lockers. I *knew* I was smart, at least in some things. I'd given up on accomplishing much in math or science, but classes like Contemporary Issues and English—these I should be good at.

But I'd blown it in English this year, too. The teacher, Ms. Morse, was young enough to be fresh from college. On the first day of class she wore an ankle-length peasant skirt and talked about literature with a dreamy look in her eye, and I felt hopeful. But then she assigned *The Crucible.* Please! I'd read that play in the seventh grade. I spent class time reading Hermann Hesse's *Narcissus and Goldmund* beneath my desk instead. Everything would have been fine if I hadn't been sitting next to stupid Troy Tunis. I got misty-eyed when Goldmund died, and Troy—who has the vocabulary of Cro-Magnon Man—sniggered, and Ms. Morse pounced. Our teacher-student relationship had gone downhill from there.

Social studies had been a disaster, too. First term I'd been required to take a course called Scottish History and Heritage, which covered both Scotland and Scottish settlement in North Carolina. Mom had latched on to this local culture stuff because she had a big hole to fill in her life. She's a reference librarian who moonlights as a certified professional genealogist, so on top of keeping her busy, these forays into all things Scottish help her work life, too. Nan had bounced along with her because she was too naive to know the score. But I wasn't ready to renounce my *real* life back in Green Bay: Catholic church, Polish food on holidays, and a second internship waiting at the local public television station. I had hated the Scottish course and limped through with a B minus.

And now I was facing a worse grade in Contemporary Issues. Suddenly my knees felt wobbly, and I slid down the locker until I reached the floor. My sophomore year in high school was almost over, and I had nothing to show for it.

I stared at a bulletin board on the opposite wall, which was covered with neon-colored posters and computer-generated notices: *Don't miss the Spring Fling!* Whatever that was. *Tryouts for summer band camp on Tuesday!* No doubt complete with bagpipes. *The debate club will meet in Mrs. Martingale's room!* No, thank you.

Suddenly I frowned. I got up and slowly peeled back the corner of a sign about cheerleading practice. Completely hidden beneath it was the notice I'd stapled up a week earlier: *Anyone interested in forming a videography club? Sharing ideas about shooting, editing, software, and equipment? Working together over the summer? If so, please sign up below.*

Three people had signed up: Steven Spielberg, Abraham Lincoln, and Mickey Mouse.

I stared at the signatures for a moment, then carefully tacked the cheerleading poster back in place. A couple of passing kids gave me curious looks, but no one stopped or spoke to me. No surprise there.

Before even moving south, I'd checked out my new school on the Web. Highland High School in Laurinburg, Scotland County, North Carolina. "Hahland Hah," as the locals say, is Home of the Fighting Scots. Home of a marching band that wears full Scottish regalia. With one mouse click a visitor to the school's home page can listen to "Scotland the Brave," the anthem of all good Scots. Which I was not.

Well, so be it. I was Tanya Zeshonski from Green Bay, Wisconsin. Tanya Zeshonski, independent filmmaker.

I slid my Panasonic from the bottom of my daypack and felt better as soon as the camera was snug against my palm. I peeked furtively around the corner. Mrs. Martingale was still working at her desk.

By holding the incriminating paper against the lockers with my left hand, I managed to pan from that scarlet F to Mrs. Martingale, walled behind her thick glasses and parrot earrings. It required a tricky zoom, but I got the shot. As the camera purred quietly, I imagined editing those frames into a demo tape about my work—perhaps for a lifetime-achievement awards ceremony. Maybe

Steven Spielberg would present the award. "She gave you an F for turning in a doc treatment?" he'd say, shaking his head. "Unbelievable! I'm glad you didn't let that stop you!"

I turned off the camera and cocooned it back in my daypack before escaping into the May sunshine. I'd missed my bus, of course. Mom wouldn't be off work for another couple of hours. Slinging my daypack over my shoulder, I headed out on the long walk home.

Chapter 4

We had an early supper that night because Mom had a doubleheader: some genealogy clients coming over at seven, and some cronies from Clan MacDonald at eight. But even when she's in a hurry, Mom always asks Nan and me about our day while we eat. Luckily, once I say, "O.K., I guess," I can usually count on Nan to fill up the rest of our allotted time. I'd have to talk to Mom about my grades at some point, but I didn't mind postponing that conversation.

"Can I call Dad?" Nan asked finally as she scraped the last trace of lime sherbet from her bowl. "I want to tell him about the dance competition, and he wasn't home over the weekend."

"Of course, dear," Mom said calmly. My mom can be a real saint.

Nan took the phone upstairs, and Mom went into the living room to get ready for the Fergusons, her clients. Not that tidying up was a big deal anymore. My dad used to move through rooms like a tornado, leaving discarded jackets and junk mail and folders spilling student work in his wake.

Mom and I kept the living room spotless because she often had clients over. It's not clear to me why so many people are interested in looking up their ancestors. I think people who live in the past are hiding from the here and now. Forward, that's my motto.

It wasn't my turn to wash dishes that evening, but since two of the people in the house had better things to do, I did them anyway. I didn't really mind; Mom had let me organize the cupboards when we moved in, and putting things back in their proper places gave me a sense of satisfaction. The world would be a better place with a bit more order.

Then I retreated to the computer, which was crunched into what used to be a pantry because the three of us shared it. I was editing some footage of a sailboat race on Lake Michigan for a documentary I was making about an all-female crew. I'd been saving money for a basic Avid software package—a truly *awesome* editing system. Still, even cheap software was fun to play around with.

I was tinkering with a dissolve when Nan walked into the pantry, holding the phone. "Dad wants to talk to you."

For a split second, like always, the world felt normal; Dad was off on a trip and calling to say good night. Then, like always, I remembered, and my stomach muscles clenched.

Worse, Nan had probably told Dad about my performance in the sword dance. She stood now with arm outstretched, phone balanced on her palm, her face bland. I pictured my paternal unit on the other end, waiting. The familiar anger began to simmer in my chest. There were things Nan didn't know about our father—things I didn't *want* her to know—and Lord Almighty, that made life hard sometimes.

I sat like a statue. She finally thrust the phone into my hand. I held it for a few seconds before pressing it to my ear. "Hello?"

"Tanya!" My dad's voice was full of false cheer. "How are you?"

"O.K., I guess."

"School's almost out, right?"

"Yeah."

"You must be looking forward to the summer. Do you have any plans?"

"Not really."

"Did you give any more thought to taking an acting workshop? There must be something in your area. I'll pay for it—"

"I don't want to take an acting workshop, Dad!" I clenched the phone so hard I thought the plastic might crack.

He drew a deep, audible breath. "I'm not saying you should commit your life to the theater. But let your old man share some of what he's learned. Getting stage experience will build your self-confidence. I'm trying to help you, Tanya."

Nan *had* told him about the sword dance. I wanted to wring her scrawny little neck.

Dad talked at me: how a skit for the Catholic men's fellowship talent show had almost done him in three years ago, how his fellow teachers had talked him into participating in the faculty performance of *"You're a Good Man, Charlie Brown"* two years ago, how good it had all been for him, blah blah blah.

"Yeah, I know, Dad," I said when he paused for breath. Dad seemed to think that message repetition would work where mere words had failed.

A pause. Then, "Would you like to come up to Wisconsin this summer?"

I thought about Wisconsin in the summer, the north-woods and the Great Lakes, and felt a lump rise in my throat.

"Did Nan tell you I just landed the lead in *Oklahoma!* at the Appleton dinner theater?" I could hear the satisfaction in his voice. "If you timed it right, you could catch a performance."

This was the price tag: applauding my dad as he took his bows, sitting beside his new wife. Unless, of course, his new wife was once again performing in the same show.

"Tanya?"

"Here's Nan again," I said, and shoved the phone into my sister's hand. She glared at me. I glared back.

After assuring Dad how much she loved him, Nan hung up and scowled. "Why are you so mean to Dad?" she asked.

"I'm not mean. I'm really tired tonight."

"It's not just tonight!" she insisted stubbornly.

"Hush!" I jerked my head toward the living room, where Mom was explaining pedigree charts or some such to her clients. Nan flounced off in a huff.

A dramatic huff. Nan was good at such things. After Dad got "bitten by the theater bug," he'd taken Nan and me to an audition for a community theater production of *Annie*. I found myself standing on a stage, the director and her cohorts invisible in the darkened auditorium. The lines I'd memorized evaporated in my brain. The simple dance steps they asked for might as well have been from classical ballet. Bottom line: I froze like a wet fish.

Nan got the part of the youngest orphan, and she loved every minute. Maybe she was too young to remember the old, normal dad—a disorganized eighth-grade geography teacher, for God's sake, who spent his evenings grading papers and complaining about apathetic students. The dad Nan knew skipped family dinner so he'd make rehearsal on time, and she was fine with that.

Once, after the proverbial excrement had hit the fan, I overheard Mom talking to a friend on the phone. She called my father's big change a "midlife crisis." In movies, the men having crises usually buy sports cars and date their twenty-something secretaries. My dad hit the stage and married the leading lady.

Just then I considered charging after Nan to set her straight. Instead I made coffee and set out sugar and cream, with small silver spoons aligned neatly next to folded napkins. The MacDonald cronies began to arrive almost as soon as Mom sent her clients on their way, and she flashed me a grateful look when she dashed into the kitchen and grabbed the tray. I spent the rest of the evening at the computer, trying to block out the sporadic bursts of conversation that penetrated through the wall:

"I'm bringing the clan pamphlets, but someone else has the castle prints. . . ."

"Last time we were next to those Lindsays, and their flag blew over and took out our awning. . . ."

"Did the brochures about the Scotland trip get back from the printer? If we don't get thirty people signed up by July 1, we'll lose our group rates. . . ."

I sighed. It was going to be one of those nights. I would kill for my own computer, locked away in the sanctity of my bedroom. I'd spent too many evenings working at the computer while Mom and her new friends discussed Scottish legend and lore in the next room. People like our creaking farmhouse because the front room dates back to the 1700s, when one of our plucky ancestors arrived in North Carolina colony and built a one-room cabin. The old homestead has been in Mom's family ever since. "This house just seems to *bless* our gatherings," a particularly over-the-top lady from Greensboro had once gushed.

That night it was harder than usual to ignore what was going on. Mom and her gang of MacDonalds were planning their participation at the Cross Creek Highland Games that coming weekend. And therein dangled my own fate. Mom and I were headed toward A Talk.

Highland Games are huge Scottish culture things, with a cultish following. They feature bizarre athletic competitions and demonstrations of Border collies herding sheep and reenactors charging about with broadswords. Stuff like that. Highland dancers compete. Pipers and pipe bands compete, too. And in North Carolina, a state that successfully lobbied the U.S. legislature to adopt a National Tartan Day, such things are not taken lightly.

It was almost eleven o'clock before I heard the assorted MacDonalds take their leave. Mom carried the coffee tray into the kitchen and set it by the sink. "Did you clean up?" she asked. "Thank you."

"Sure. How did things go with that couple who hired you? Did you find any skeletons in their closet?"

"With the Fergusons? Not really, unless you count a great-uncle who married his housekeeper." Mom sank into a chair and rested her elbows on the table. "They want me to do some more work, flesh out some of the other lines."

"That's great, Mom."

"Mrs. Ferguson is going to call a cousin in Nebraska and see if he has any records for me to start from. They're coming to the Highland Games this weekend, and she said she'd stop by the tent and let me know."

I waited for it.

"Tanya, about the Games—"

"I really don't want to go." I tried to sound calm. Not petulant. I hate petulance, most especially in myself.

"Aren't you going to get back in the saddle, so to speak? One misstep at a dance competition doesn't mean anything! Don't you want to try again?"

I distinctly did not.

"I think it would do you good." Mom looked at me, worry creasing her forehead.

"Can't I just stay home?" Mom had come up with this maniacal plan to *camp* at the Cross Creek Highland Games. If I went, I'd be trapped in Scottish purgatory for the whole weekend.

The very idea made me want to cry. In fact, tears might have done the trick with Mom. Ever since the blowup in Wisconsin, she'd been urging me to cry, to "let everything out," with a repetition that came to pluck on my nerves like a bagpipe's drone. I hadn't cried since before my father left, and if I could muster some water-works now, it would be impressive. I gave it a try. Nothing came.

"I'm worried about you, Tanya," Mom said quietly. "You've bottled everything up inside. You need an outlet."

"I have an outlet. Videography."

"Videography is a wonderful but very solitary pursuit."

I thought about my attempt to form a videography club. "I like making documentaries."

"I know, dear, but I think you need to interact with other people."

She said that a lot these days, too. I used to remind her that I had interacted with other people back in Green Bay, but that only made her pinch her lips and get snippy. "I am doing my very best for this family, Tanya," she'd say with two sudden spots of scarlet burning high on her cheeks, and sometimes a glint of tears in *her* eyes. "Nanag is settling in here because she's making the effort to. If you would just try . . ."

Well, I had. I had tried the sword dance. I had tried to make friends at Highland High School. I had tried to do a creative project for my Contemporary Issues class.

"Let's make a deal," Mom said finally. "I want you to come to the Highland Games this weekend with me and Nan. You can try again in the dance competition, or you can help at the clan tent with me, or you can sightsee—anything you want, as long as you give it a fair try. After that, if you truly don't want to go to any more Games, I'll let you stay home."

I wanted to argue. I'm fifteen! I wanted to say. Old enough to make my own choices! Old enough to do what I want!

But Mom had this pleading look in her eyes, and I couldn't help remembering all she'd been through in the last year or so. How much she'd suffered. How hard *she'd* tried.

"O.K., Mom," I said at last. "It's a deal."

Chapter 5

On Friday afternoon Mom picked Nan and me up from school, the car already packed. We sped to the Highland Games, made a cursory stab at setting up our campsite, and then lit out for Clan Tent MacDonald.

Clan tents form the heart of every Highland Games. Every clan organization that can scrape up the entrance fee reserves tent space. The clan tents are places for clan members to gather, and for nonmembers to learn more about the individual clans. At the Cross Creek Games, clan row was set nicely in a grove of trees. A big sign saying "Glen O' the Clans" pointed the way. Worker bees in a bewildering kaleidoscope of tartans flitted back and forth among the pines, shouting greetings, hauling boxes of brochures, nailing up signs and banners, spreading tablecloths, arranging displays.

And spying. In this weekend of competitions, clan societies compete for one of the most coveted prizes of all: the Best Clan Tent award. As I understand it, judging is based on concrete benchmarks like "best display of clan pride" and "best use of tartan" and "best explanation of clan heritage." I could see clan members casually scoping out the competition as Nan and I followed Mom toward the Clan MacDonald tent.

There are many variations of MacDonald tartans, and the tent was draped in yards of a plaid even more garish than Nan's kilt, with red and black and blue and green all clamoring for top billing. Against that backdrop a little knot of MacDonalds were already quibbling about tent décor. "I was going to hang the clan map over the display table," one was saying.

"But the portrait of Bonnie Prince Charlie should be front and center," another MacDonald insisted.

I recognized the portrait because I'd had to write a report about the man who'd returned to Scotland from exile in 1745, raised an army of Highlanders, and led them to a massacre at Culloden Moor. *That* unleashed a storm of genocidal atrocities upon the Highland people. "Ah, Bonnie Prince C.," I said under my breath. "The incompetent and self-absorbed heir of a deposed king."

All heads swiveled toward me. Evidently my voice had been louder than intended. Mom gave me A Look.

"Sorry," I said brightly. "I'll just help with the boxes." Cardboard cartons and plastic storage bins littered the ground. Obviously, the MacDonalds were not well organized.

This was a job for Tanya Zeshonski. I didn't have proper materials—colored markers, sticky notes, index cards—but I made do. After stashing my own storage tub of extra videotapes and batteries, I soon had books about clan history arranged on the display table in alphabetical order, by author. Brochures got fanned on the other end. Application forms for clan membership were stacked nearby, with pens ready. I filed extras neatly in boxes and printed the contents of each on the outside. Cartons I thought warranted quick access were hidden beneath the table. The rest I lugged behind the tent, out of sight.

"You could help, you know," I said pointedly to Nan as I staggered past with a box. She'd made herself comfortable in a lawn chair and had disappeared into a novel. The cover art—manly men in old-style kilts—suggested historical fiction.

"This is too exciting," she said, her gaze not leaving the page. "You should read it when I'm done, Tanya. It's about the MacDonalds and an old feud—"

"That's O.K." I eased the box down and went back for another. I'd had enough Scottish history crammed down my throat.

Finally I caught Mom's attention. "Let me show you where everything is," I told her, and gave the tour. "And if you keep track of pamphlet and T-shirt inventory on these cards," I added, "you'll know when you're running low and won't get caught empty-handed."

Mom gave my shoulder a quick squeeze. "You are a marvel, Tanya. Thank you."

I had to smile past a lump in my throat, because I had

one of those sudden flashbacks that still popped up when I least expected them. The summer after eighth grade my dad spent a week in Milwaukee at some teacher training thing, and I'd decided to surprise him by organizing his study. I spent the whole week clipping articles, sorting through stacks of magazines, rolling maps. I even cross-referenced his files using colored file folders. "Surprise!" I said, when he saw the room for the first time. "You can actually see the carpet now. Do you like it?" He nodded slowly. I'd waited for more, waited for him to tell me I was a marvel. "Sure, Tanya," he had said finally. "Sure."

Forward. "You're welcome," I told Mom. "See you later. Come on, Nan. It's time to go find the dance area."

Nan and I left Mom with the MacDonalds and headed toward the dance arena. Nan zoomed ahead. I trailed grimly behind, the hanger bearing my kilt slung over one shoulder.

I hadn't planned to ever dance on stage again. But I had underestimated Miss Janet from the Flora MacDonald School of Highland Dance. She'd come by our house unannounced on Wednesday evening while Nan was off at that dance clinic in Fayetteville.

Miss Janet was a thin, forty-something, steel-haired woman who often shouted, "Dance for the joy of it!" in the middle of class. I can't say we'd ever connected on a personal level. But I did like her, which made it hard to admit that I'd been taking dance classes for almost a year and had never felt anything remotely like joy.

"I stopped by to make sure you're still planning to participate this weekend," Miss Janet had said.

I studied the wall over her shoulder. "Um, I don't think so, Miss Janet."

She shook her head. "You had a rocky start at competition, I know. It's unfortunate that the sword dance was first round. If you could have started with the fling, you would have been fine."

"It's not just that," I tried. "It's—"

"I should have prepared you better." Miss Janet rubbed her forehead. "I'm afraid I let you down."

"No, Miss Janet, that's not true! I just . . . um . . . I don't think Highland dance is really my thing. Especially competition—"

"Competition." Miss Janet, who had won more than a few trophies in her day, waved that aside. "Competition exists to provide a personal challenge, which can be rewarding. But you must dance again for the pure pleasure of it."

Pure pleasure of it? Was the woman insane? I couldn't imagine anything less pleasurable than the thought of facing my swords again. Unless it was to fall upon them.

Mom hadn't said a word, and I made the mistake of looking at her for help. Hope shone in her face. *I want you to be O.K.,* that look said. *I want you to have an outlet. I want you to fit in, make friends, be involved.* No help there.

I did *not* want to dance at the Cross Creek Highland Games. But neither could I stomach the image of Miss Janet and my mom lying awake at night thinking they'd failed me. So against the frantic screams of my better judgment, I packed my kilt and ghillies.

While last Saturday's competition had been small—just between three dance schools—many more dancers would be involved this time, and the competition would last all weekend. After the Highland dance competitions, the more advanced dancers would also compete in the less percussive dances like the Scottish lilt or Blue Bonnets, or character dances like the jig and the sailor's hornpipe. The first rounds began that afternoon. A low, temporary stage had been constructed for the dancers—mostly girls, but a few boys, too.

"You should have come to the clinic," Nan said for the eleventh time. "I got some good advice."

"Come on." I tugged her to a quiet corner in one of the tents provided for changing clothes. "You get dressed first, and I'll do your hair outside where I can see what I'm doing." I dropped my dance bag on the floor and balanced the hanger over a handy rod suspended from the ridgepole.

Nan squirmed into her kilt. "I think it's good that the Highland fling is first round today," she said. "Don't you think it's good?"

The Highland fling is the most famous of all Highland

dances, supposedly first performed by victorious warriors. They danced on the round shields they carried, called targes. Needless to say, the Highland fling doesn't cover a whole lot of ground.

There are no automatic outs in the Highland fling like there are in the sword dance. I could dance the fling. I could make Mom and Nan and Miss Janet happy.

"Don't you want to get dressed?" Nan asked anxiously. She pulled on her plaid socks and hid the skinny elastic bands under the cuffs.

I heard the first screech of a bagpipe and cringed. "I've got time. I want to make sure you're all set first." When Nan was suitably attired, I settled her on a folding chair outside and tackled her hair.

I was poking in a final hairpin when the chill hit me, so hard I shuddered. One instant I was fine; the next instant every muscle in my body went rigid.

"Ow!" Nan complained. Then her expression cleared, and she stared at Christina Campbell, who had appeared at her elbow. "Oh, *hi!*"

"Hi, Nanag," Christina Campbell said. She hadn't changed yet, and in running shoes and faded jeans, with her mousy hair down, I almost didn't recognize her.

Then she looked at me. "Hi, Tanya. It's nice to see you again."

I gulped for air. "Hi."

"Good luck today," Christina told Nan, her tone warm as honey. "And you, too," she added politely to me, although I could tell from her expression that she felt my frost and didn't understand it. I didn't understand it, either.

"Thanks, Christina!" Nan said. "I'll be watching you, especially in the Highland fling. That's my favorite. That and the sword dance—"

"Since the Highland fling and the sword dance were traditionally only performed by men," I said, "our participation in this competition perpetuates a myth."

Nan froze. Christina's mouth twisted into a frown. "See you around," she said, and walked on past.

"What is the *matter* with you!" Nan wailed, turning on me. "Christina is *nice!* Why are you so *mean* all the time?"

Before I could find an answer, two chattering girls paused nearby. "Hey, Nanag!" one called. "We're going to register and get our competition numbers."

"I'll come with you," Nan told them. After shooting me a look that suggested I'd kicked a kitten, she caught up with her friends.

I watched her skinny backside until it had disappeared into the crowd. For another long moment I stood in the doorway of the changing tent and stared at my kilt, still hung neatly in its garment bag. Then I walked away.

I hurried through the parking lot, which was a big field rapidly filling with cars. This was farm country—no handy cabs or metro buses in sight. Volunteers in kilts and Cross Creek Highland Games polo shirts waved the stream into tidy rows. I plowed down one of the lanes, passing minivans with bumper stickers that shouted slogans like "God Made Scots a Wee Bit Better" and "Old Pipers Don't Die, They Just Drone On."

I headed for a little lake I remembered seeing beyond the farthest row of parked cars, and plopped down beside it. It wasn't actually a lake. I was born in northeastern Wisconsin—I know lakes. This was more of a pond. A little pond, covered with green scum.

That's what I felt like. Pond scum.

I wrapped my arms around my legs and rested my cheek on my knees. I wanted to cry, but the tears wouldn't come. I closed my eyes and tried to let my mind go blank. The pond scum smelled faintly of . . . well, of pond scum, but it wasn't annoying. Perhaps I could just stay here for the next three days. . . .

The sudden blare of bagpipes almost jolted me from my skin. Friggin' H! That was just *it.* Jumping to my feet, I whirled on the culprit: a dark-haired boy about my age, standing back by the cars. He wore a kilt and jacket and one of those silly hats they call a glengarry.

It was the same guy who had played at my disastrous competition.

"Hey!" I yelled. He didn't hear me at first—no surprise there—so I marched closer and bellowed: *"Hey!"*

He stopped, and the wail tapered off discordantly. "What?"

"What are you doing?"

He frowned. "Don't I know you from somewhere?"

"No," I said firmly. "What are you doing?"

The piper looked at me as if I were the victim of a poorly performed lobotomy. "Playing the bagpipes."

I closed my eyes for a moment and asked for strength. "I *know* that. Do you have to do it right here?"

"Yes."

"Look. I came here for a few minutes of peace and quiet in the great outdoors." I gestured grandly at the pond.

"So did I," he said reasonably. "I wanted to practice away from the crowd. I'm playing solo in Junior Novice, and it's my first competition."

"But I was here first. Can't you just . . . just move along somewhere else?"

"I like the pond."

This was absurd. I felt like a tired three-year-old, too stubborn to back down. I squinted at him and was struck again by his coloring. "Are you from around here?"

"I was born on the Isla de Culebra, in Puerto Rico."

Puerto Rico . . . I searched my mental database of research done for the Contemporary Issues project. "Hey . . . does your family fish? Have you gotten involved in any of the disputes between environmentalists and the companies interested in offshore oil?"

"You know about that?" He looked gratified.

I felt a twist of genuine excitement. "Yeah. It would be a *perfect* subject for a documentary. For PBS. I'm a documentarian," I added.

He looked suitably impressed . . . or at least startled. Or perhaps just dubious. It was hard to tell. "Really? For PBS?"

"Well . . . I was. Before I had to move to North Carolina. I'll get back to it when I can."

I left it at that. The truth was I'd landed my first internship at the public television station in Green Bay the last year I went to school there, part of an "Experience the Workplace" initiative funded by a local bank to improve its image after a vice president absconded to Mexico with a bunch of funds and the president's wife.

I spent most of those three months at WPNE making photocopies and logging tape. The producers sometimes let me sit in on Avid edit sessions, although it quickly became clear that my creative insight wasn't welcome. In my last week there, a producer had taken me along on a field shoot when her normal PA—that's Production Assistant—came down with strep throat. She was making a documentary about migrant families in Wisconsin, and I thought I had hit the big time until I realized we were only shooting scenic shots, called B-Roll, that day. No clandestine forays into the dark underbelly of migrant camps for gritty interviews. I tended the cut sheet, which is even less interesting than logging tape, and my name didn't show up in the program credits.

But that experience hadn't dampened my drive to make documentaries. I'd known what I wanted to do ever since I was ten and my parents got a cheap camcorder to record family vacations and birthday parties and stuff like that. I picked it up for the first time on a rocky beach in Door County. When I looked through the monitor, I focused in on a boy playing Frisbee with his golden retriever, and I thought, I'm the first person to ever see this movie. The boy was throwing the Frisbee into the lake for his dog to fetch, and one time the wind caught it and the dog had to swim so far I could scarcely breathe. But the dog made it back to shore safely, and I caught the whole thing on tape. There was something powerful, almost magical, about that experience.

A good documentarian is always on the lookout for contacts and stories. "So . . . what's your name?" I asked.

"Miguel Moreno. What's yours?"

"Tanya Zeshonski. Would you be willing to talk with me about Puerto Rico?"

Considering that I was offering him—at least in theory—a rare opportunity to speak to the world about the injustice being wrought by greedy oil-sniffing imperialists, he looked surprisingly underwhelmed. "I don't think so. I'm not in that place right now."

"That place?"

"I want to *practice* right now. The bagpipes? Remember? Besides, that's not really your story to tell, is it."

I'm sure no one ever says that to Ken Burns. "What?"

He shrugged. "Why don't you make a documentary about something from your own life? Do one about the Highland Games." He waved toward the festival grounds.

I rolled my eyes. "Highland Games mean nothing to me. Most of the Highland heritage types I've seen are more interested in cozy nostalgia than researching the past. I'm not interested in documenting a hokey celebration. I thought you might be interested in helping me expose the truth about—"

"No—thank—you!" A flicker of annoyance crossed his face. "Right now, I need to practice. I'm on in half an hour. I'm *competing.*"

"Well, find another spot to practice," I snapped.

Real anger sparked in those dark eyes, and for a moment I thought—hoped—Miguel was going to lash back. Then his face closed. He squared his shoulders and lifted his chin. "I want to practice near the pond," he said with enormous dignity. "I am *going* to practice right here."

"Then—just—*fine.* You can have the scummy old pond."

He settled the bag under his left arm, with the three pipes splayed over his shoulder, and started playing a jig as I stomped away. I was halfway down one of the rows of cars before I realized that my fists were clenched, and my jaw, too. Something inside my chest hurt. It was hard to breathe. I wondered if I was having a stroke. Did fifteen-year-olds ever have strokes? It seemed very likely.

Chapter 6

I managed to hang on to self-righteous indignation as I stalked through the parking field. I ended up right back where I didn't want to be: the festival grounds.

I stood at the entrance, considering. The Highland Games covered several acres. A field the size of a football stadium filled the center. Food vendors lined the western border, and other merchants the north. In addition to the dance pavilion, activity tents and stages dotted the grounds. The camping area filled the northeast corner, beyond the clan tents.

None of it called to me, so I wandered. At the open-air folk stage a kilted man was playing a guitar and singing a sad lament about Bonnie Prince Charlie. A perfect example of what I was telling Miguel! See, this whole Highland heritage thing—in large part, it's a fabrication. A *myth*. All Scottish people are *not* Highlanders. All Scottish people did *not* fight with Bonnie Prince Charlie—in fact, a bunch fought against him, and most tried to sit the whole mess out.

I stifled the urge to put my fingers in my ears. The

Highland heritage phenomenon is all very hard on a documentarian.

Then I sighed and turned away. I *was* turning into a witch. I was hypercritical, and I'd been rude to Miguel on top of being rude to Christina and hurtful to Nan. Maybe, I thought hopefully, it was the ungodly climate, which was not designed for cheeseheads from Wisconsin. Maybe all that heat and humidity just got trapped inside and had to bubble out somehow. Still, it was unsettling.

Chocolate. I needed chocolate, most preferably entwined with peanut butter in some manner. A quick scan of the food vendors' tents reinforced what I already knew: chocolate is not a traditional Scottish food. I am descended from people who thrived on haggis and oatmeal and, when times got bad, blood from their cattle. Haggis is made by mixing a sheep's heart and liver with oatmeal before packing it into the sheep's stomach for baking, so in my opinion that reflected bad times, too.

I settled for shortbread, the one nonhorrid bit of Scottish culinary tradition. Scottish shortbread is basically made from equal parts of butter and sugar, with just enough flour to bind it all together. As I finished off my third piece, I wondered what to do next. It was the kind of spring day event planners light candles in cathedrals for, and I was free.

Free—*right.* It was only Friday afternoon. I may have

turned my back on the dance competition, but I was stuck in a tartanized Disneyland. Bagpipes screeched from every direction. I'd likely go stark raving mad before Sunday night.

Licking my fingers, I stopped outside the Youth Activities Tent for a moment, listening to a storyteller entertain a dozen or so kids with a tale of Scottish glory. "William Wallace is Scotland's *greatest* hero," she said breathlessly. "In the battle at Stirling Bridge, *wa-a-a-y* back in 1297, William Wallace and his Scots defeated the *huge* English army. That's why we call him *Braveheart.*"

She was *wa-a-a-y* too melodramatic for my tastes. I ducked inside.

The tent, about the size of my living room, was largely deserted. An elderly gentleman wearing Scottish regalia involving a particularly ugly tartan hurried forward to meet me. "Did you bring a project for the judging?" he asked with a smile that crinkled his face. He reminded me of my father's father, dead for almost two years now, and I swallowed hard. Grandpa Zeshonski wouldn't have been caught dead in a kilt. He'd been a butcher, known throughout Brown County for both his Polish smoked pork sausage, called kielbasa, and the huge shrine to the Madonna watching over his shop. If Grandpa was keeping an eye on us from heaven, I suspect he was equally horrified by his son's behavior and his granddaughters' new affiliation with Presbyterianism.

The kilted man cleared his throat politely. "Oh . . . I beg your pardon?" I managed.

"The judging," he said again, gesturing to tables lining the tent walls. A sign hung above the nearest: Our Highland Heritage—Student Projects.

I stepped closer and surveyed the offerings: A photo essay about raising Border collies mounted on blaze orange tagboard. A display of bits of yarn dyed by walnuts and mullein leaves and other natural materials. A Magic Marker portrait of Bonnie Prince Charlie. A neatly printed essay titled "Voyage of the *Thistle.*" Thistles are held sacred as the national emblem of Scotland. This particular Thistle had evidently been a ship.

"The *Thistle* is considered the *Mayflower* of North Carolina Scots," I read aloud. "It brought the celebrated group of 350 Scots who traveled from Argyllshire, in southwest Scotland, to Cape Fear, North Carolina, in the eighteenth century." I wondered what those first emigrants would have thought if they could have known what their arrival would spawn.

The old gentleman loomed over my shoulder. "Are you participating in the competition?" he asked hopefully.

"Um, no." He looked so disappointed that I felt compelled to add, "I didn't know about it, you see, and—"

"But it's not too late!" He beamed. "The deadline for entering isn't until three o'clock on Sunday afternoon."

"Well, I'll think about it." I was saved from further equivocation by the arrival of a gap-toothed boy carrying a shoebox diorama of the Loch Ness monster. Nessie reared her clay head from a loch of blue tissue paper. The boy's mother snapped pictures while the boy proudly offered the diorama to the coordinator.

I backed away, then darted outside. I paused. H'm. That Scottish mom . . . I knew the type. And she reminded me that I really shouldn't put off checking in with my own. I'd lay good money on the likelihood that Nan had already informed our mother, in torrid emotional detail, that I'd fled from the dance arena once again.

The shortbread vendor beckoned. Figuratively, that is. I ate two more pieces of shortbread. Thus fortified, I trudged toward the clan tents.

I found the MacDonald crew still busy. Mom was appraising two men perched on ladders with a huge banner spread between them. They had wisely opted to complete setup before shucking their trousers. "Doug, your corner needs to come up a bit," Mom called. "No! Too much! Down again! *Yes!* Perfect!"

While Doug and friend nailed the banner between two obliging trees, I presented myself. "Hey, Mom."

She whirled, and for just a second I saw the glowing smile that transformed her freckled face whenever she hung out with kith and kin. Then it was replaced by that universal look of sorrowful parental concern that drives kids nuts. "Oh—Tanya, dear." She put a hand on my shoulder, searching my face. "Nanag brought your kilt back, and she said—"

"I'm fine," I said shortly, envisioning my pursuit of darling Nan with a Highland pistol in my hand. Or perhaps a broadsword. I could do a lot of damage with a broadsword.

"I'm sure it was just nerves again, dear."

"Mom."

"Skipping the Highland fling this afternoon doesn't mean you can't compete tomorrow—"

"*Mom!*" I took a deep breath. "I'm done dancing," I said in a calmer voice. "I'm not going to compete."

Her shoulders slumped. "But, Tanya—"

Mom bit off her protest as a woman bearing a startling resemblance to Mrs. Santa Claus, but in tartan, joined us. "Mary," she said, looking worried, "have you seen the Gordon tent?"

"With the wooden backdrop painted to look like a castle fortress?" Mom nodded.

"It's got me worried."

"It's a nice touch," Mom allowed, "but I'm still confident. We're unveiling Rosemary's cross-stitch of the clan motto this weekend. It's an eye-popper."

The MacDonald Clan motto is "By Sea and by Land." I simply could not wait to see it presented in cross-stitch.

After the woman moved back out of earshot, Mom turned to me again. "Tanya, I'm worried about you."

"Mother, I said I'm *fine!*"

She chewed her lip, regarding me. I was struck with a sudden mental image of her wearing her lavender bathrobe, and I looked away, swallowing everything I wanted to say.

Dad had given her that bathrobe after they spent a weekend in some swank hotel in Chicago for their anniversary. Mom had fallen in love with the thick terry robes provided for the guests, and Dad tracked one down and gave it to her for Christmas. I hardly ever saw her in it, actually, because Mom is not a lounge-around kind of person. She was always dressed before Nan and I got out of bed in the morning, and didn't change into pajamas until she was ready to get into bed at night.

But after Dad abandoned us, she began showing up at the breakfast table wearing that robe. She'd sit slumped in a chair drinking coffee and staring at the place mat while Nan and I gulped bowls of granola as fast as we could before beating it to the bus stop. Then came the day when I got home from school and found Mom sitting in the living room, staring at some sleazy talk show on TV. Now, please understand, I was eight before Mom even clued me in to the fact that PBS wasn't the only network in existence. But there was Mom, watching commercial television at three o'clock in the afternoon . . . wearing that lavender bathrobe. I don't think she even heard me come in. For a long time I stood in the doorway, wondering if this was how it was going to be.

And that's how it *was,* for a while. But somehow she managed to get moving again . . . right on down to North Carolina. The lavender bathrobe ended up at Goodwill, traded in for a kilt of MacDonald plaid. That's why I truly tried to cut her some slack on this Scottish stuff.

"I had hoped . . . ," she said slowly. "Well, anyway. All right. What are you going to do with yourself all weekend, then? Do you want to help out at the tent with me?"

I glanced at the display table, where two women were wrangling over the placement of Rosemary's cross-stitched motto. "I don't think so."

"Tanya, I don't see how Nan and I can enjoy ourselves this weekend, knowing that you're drifting about without an activity to engage your—"

"I have an activity."

She blinked. "You do? What?"

"I'm going to enter the student projects competition. The theme is 'Our Highland Heritage.'"

I don't know which one of us was more surprised by that announcement.

"You are?" she asked after a moment.

I nodded.

"What are you going to do?"

"I'm going to make a documentary. I just came to pick up another battery."

Mom mulled that over. "But won't you want to edit the tape? You're not going to turn in raw footage, are you?"

She was thinking faster than I was. I hated when she did that. "Well," I hedged, "I'm going to shoot what I need this weekend and *then* make a documentary. I'll enter it in the competition at the next Games we go to."

The suspicion faded, replaced with a tentative smile. "That's a lovely idea! I can set up some interviews, if you'd like."

"I'll let you know!" I nodded vigorously. "I'm going to start with B-Roll first. You know, scenic shots I can use with voice-over." I was itching to get out of there.

Mom followed me around the public space to the area behind the tent where I'd stashed my camera and extra supplies, and where various MacDonalds had stored their beverages of choice in coolers. "Get some footage of Nanag, will you?" Mom rummaged among her things, then straightened with a tartan sash in her hand. "And here. You'll feel more a part of things if you wear this." She positioned the sash over my right shoulder and knotted it above my left hip. Beaming, she surveyed her handiwork.

"I'm not sure how the Packers would feel about this." I indicated the football team's logo on my shirt.

"Mary!" Doug burst around the corner of the tent. "Do you know where the clan history booklets got to? I've got an elderly couple up front asking questions. . . ."

Had he even looked? "I put inventory lists on the

boxes," I began, but Mom planted a kiss on my cheek and dashed back to the front lines.

I whipped off the sash and tossed it into the bin of Mom's things. Armed with a pen and notepad, camera, and spare tapes and batteries, I headed out to make a documentary.

Chapter 7

The student competition idea was, of course, completely bogus—nothing more than a desperate gamble to get Mom off my case. But as I wandered back through the trees, I realized that I might be on to something. I could make a brilliant documentary about the Cross Creek Highland Games.

When I emerged from clan row, I headed for the bleachers around the main field. The sports competitions hadn't begun yet, so the stands were pretty much deserted. I needed a few minutes to collect my thoughts, scribble some notes. By the time I'd made a list of shots I wanted to get, a lanky woman in faded jeans had taken the field with a small herd of sheep and a panting Border collie. Perfect! The obligatory demonstration of sheepherding.

I spent some time getting good B-Roll of the demonstration, including a stretch on my belly for a dog's-eye view. That gave me quite a bit of sheep butt, actually, but that's what editing is for.

I hadn't been back on the bench for more than a

minute when someone plopped down beside me. "Hey," Miguel said.

"Hey." I looked at him sideways.

"I'm unarmed." He spread his hands. "I left my pipes in the car."

I felt heat slide up my cheeks. "Look, I didn't mean to be rude. I had a headache."

"I remembered why you look familiar," he announced. "Highland High School, right? Last Saturday?"

Great. "Thanks for reminding me!"

He looked irritated. "You were the one glaring at me when I was leaving. What was that all about?"

As if he didn't know! I changed topic. "How did your competition go?"

"I screwed up twice." He shrugged. "The march I played has some tricky strikes."

I had no idea what that meant. "Oh. I'm, um, sorry."

"Oh, well. I'm in a pipe band, too. Grade five."

"Is that good?"

"It's the bottom level," he admitted cheerfully. "But we have a good time. We're hoping to move to grade four one day. Anyway, our first round is tomorrow. That should be fun."

Below us, the collie was running the sheep ragged. I stared at Miguel's knees, which were decidedly spindly. Guys that skinny really shouldn't wear kilts. "Doesn't it bother you that you screwed up?"

"Not really. I'm just learning. It's really challenging to keep the bag filled and the tone even, and get the fingerings right."

How can it not bother you? I thought. "Miguel, I hope you don't mind me asking, but what are you doing here, anyway?" I pushed a strand of hair out of my eyes.

"I spend summers with my grandma in Fayetteville. I came a couple weeks early this year."

"Is she Scottish?" I'm no expert, but Miguel looked pretty whole-cloth Latino to me.

"Her grandmother was." He turned to look at me and snorted with laughter.

"What?" I demanded.

"I can tell what you're thinking. How did someone from Puerto Rico end up playing the bagpipes?"

"Well . . ."

"Look, you don't even *like* bagpipe music, so what's the big deal? I'm not Celtic enough for you?"

"That—that's not it!" I stammered. "I just can't figure out why you *want* to. I'm only here because I don't have a choice."

"My grandmother joined her clan society after my grandfather died. She enjoys it. Last year we went to a bunch of Games together. Since I'm not here for the school year, I don't know many kids. I met some pipers, and they invited me to learn. I thought it would be fun."

"But don't you think all this stuff is kinda . . . dumb?"

He leaned back, almost lost his balance, flailed wildly, and finally settled against the bleacher bench behind him. "No. Why should I? I've got some Scottish blood. I can feel it. I'm as proud of that as I am of my Puerto Rican heritage—"

"You can *feel* it?"

"Can't you?"

"Good Lord, no."

This guy was Looney Tunes. I couldn't think of anything else to say. On the field, the lanky woman was trying to catch her dog, who had evidently decided that he'd been born to race back and forth to the sound of applause.

Then Miguel tapped the camcorder in my lap. "Whatcha doin' with that?"

"Making a documentary," I said crisply. "I'm going to compare what happens at a Games like this with the realities of Scottish history and culture. Explore why people feel the need to romanticize their history."

His black eyebrows drew together. "What is the matter with you?"

"Nothing! I just want to make a good film. My premise is that Highland Games are mostly nostalgic fabrications of what people *want* Highland heritage to be."

"Why do you care? Why can't you just let people enjoy themselves?"

"A documentary has to have a point. You have to

raise questions. Give viewers something to think about."
I believed that in an artistic sense, but there was even more
to it. I wanted to get into a top film program after high
school. I'd been searching for the makings of a truly good
documentary, with an eye to getting it aired on local cable
or even local public television. I needed a demo tape with
a variety of clips to promote my talents, but a broadcast
documentary would give a lot of weight to any college
application. And this was the best concept I'd come up
with yet.

Miguel still looked skeptical. "I'm not going to say
what's right and wrong," I said defensively. "Just lay
things out and let viewers decide."

"Uh-huh," he said in a tone that seemed calculated
to annoy.

"See down there?" I pointed at the Border collie.
"The Highlanders didn't raise sheep until *after* getting
their butts kicked at the battle of Culloden. The British
shipped flocks in because they wanted to erase the
Highlanders' way of life. Ever hear of the Clearances?
With the agricultural system in upheaval, thousands of
people got kicked off their farms by greedy landlords. The
poor people either starved or had to start over somewhere else. Sheep had a lot to do with mass emigration,
and now they're celebrated as an important part of
Scottish culture!"

Miguel rubbed his nose thoughtfully. "For someone

who seems to hate all things Scottish, you sure know a lot about Scottish history."

"Not by choice," I said briefly, not willing to be diverted. "What's your clan?"

"Armstrong. We're from the Lowlands—"

"Ha!" *Now* I had him. "Lowlanders!"

"So?"

"So in the eighteenth century, your ancestors despised mine. They called my ancestors cattle thieves and wouldn't have worn a plaid if their life depended on it and—and didn't speak a *word* of Gaelic and—"

"You're proving my point." Miguel nodded, looking satisfied.

"*What?* What point is that?"

"You seemed to take an instant dislike to me. You glared at me the first time I saw you at that school, and you were nasty back by the pond before. I couldn't figure that out, but now I get it."

I crossed my arms. "Well, do clue me in."

"It's genetic. You're obviously of Highlander stock. I'm from a Border clan."

"I didn't know that until this minute!"

"Not consciously. But on a deeper level—"

"That's crazy!"

"It's an accepted theory, and one I happen to believe in," Miguel said loftily. "Haven't you ever heard of genetic memory? Ancestral memory, some people call it."

"First of all, that's just—just—just *nuts*. Second, I'm half Polish, and you're—what, one-eighteenth Scottish or something?"

Miguel gave me a calm smile. "That doesn't matter. It's in the genes."

I rubbed my temples and closed my eyes for a moment. I hadn't had so much one-on-one conversation with a boy my age since leaving Green Bay, and what did I get? A skinny bagpipes-playing Puerto Rican New Ager who might be on drugs.

My reverie was broken by the wail of bagpipes. While Miguel and I had been arguing, the shepherd lady had finally marshaled her collie and ewes back into her SUV and driven away. Now a pipe band marched onto the field.

"Ah," Miguel sighed, instantly diverted. His toe began to tap against the bench. "Doesn't that music make you want to do a Highland fling?"

"It makes me want to fling something," I muttered, but I don't think he heard.

Chapter 8

I left Miguel watching the pipe band, and killed some time shooting B-Roll. I found a wealth of good shots: A christening ceremony for a squalling baby wearing a plaid gown. A contingent of reenactors of the 42nd Royal Highland Regiment ("The Famed Black Watch," according to their brochure) setting up their camp. A man demonstrating the process of putting on a traditional plaid—not the prim tailored kind men wear today, but the Braveheart kind. I hadn't known the expression "the whole nine yards" came from wrapping a great kilt around oneself.

I grabbed a good spot in the front row of the main field bleachers at six o'clock for the opening ceremony and Parade of Tartans. These parades are ritual events at Highland Games. Accompanied by the omnipresent bagpipes, representatives of each clan march around the field in Highland dress, carrying tartan banners. As each clan goes by, people in the stands having some connection—however slight—to that clan whoop and screech and applaud. Clan Cameron led this year's parade, an honor bestowed because they won *last* year's parade competition. I'm not sure, but I'm guessing the criteria had something to do with marching well, exhibiting clan pride, etc., etc.

After the Camerons, the parade was arranged alphabetically, so Clan Armstrong passed early on. Miguel marched by in all his Latino splendor, with a white-haired woman on his arm, both grinning. He spotted me and waved. I was so startled it took me a moment to raise a hand in return. I hoped he saw it.

The MacDonald contingent was large, as usual. It's sort of an umbrella clan, because long ago a lot of other families turned to the MacDonald chief for protection. That Doug fellow had changed into full Highland regalia and led the way carrying a big pennant that said "By Sea and by Land." I spotted Mom walking proudly in her plaid skirt and sash and beret. Nan marched with her, wearing her kilt and dance vest. I immortalized them both on videotape.

The opening ceremonies concluded with pomp and prayer and an announcement that a blue Toyota Camry parked near the vendor area had its lights on. After everyone dispersed, I went back to clan row and got some shots of the MacDonald tent. The dappled light beneath the trees presented a challenge, but I shot Rosemary's cross-stitched motto, and five generations of one MacDonald branch posed proudly in front of the banner, and some of the visitors who lingered to listen to MacDonald tales (sometimes) and tell their own (much more often).

Mom enthusiastically handled all questions about genealogical research, even the inevitable claims from MacDonald wannabes. "My mother was born a MacDonald," an elderly woman in too-tight orange shorts announced. "I believe we're descended from Flora MacDonald. As a young woman she helped Bonnie Prince Charlie escape Scotland after the massacre at Culloden, you know."

"Yes, I know," Mom said brightly. "But—"

"And later, she and her husband moved to North Carolina," the woman persisted. "My people have lived here forever. I'm sure that's our branch."

"Actually," Mom said, still chipper, "as you probably know, Flora and her husband switched loyalty during the American Revolution and supported the British army. That made life a tad uncomfortable, and two years later they fled to Canada. So we don't believe there are any local descendants. But I'm *sure* your line is equally fascinating, and if you want some help with research . . ." Somehow Mom ended up with a customer despite bursting the Flora MacDonald bubble.

Nan showed up as I was putting the camcorder in its bag. "How'd you do?" I asked, by way of making up.

"Miss Janet says my turnout is getting better," Nan replied, by way of letting me know she'd forgiven me. Then she planted herself in front of me and said, "Tanya, there's an exhibition Highland fling scheduled for Sunday morning. It's not competition, just for fun."

I shook my head. "I don't think—"

"Oh, *please?* Will you at least dance *that* with me?"

The expression on her face—pleading and hopeful at the same time—did me in. "O.K.," I said, sighing. "O.K., sure."

She smiled as if I'd promised the moon and went to help Mom at the booth.

I leaned against a tree and waited for the day to end. Looking at my watch every three minutes did little to speed that process. But finally seven-thirty came, the official closing time, and the last visitors straggled away. "That's it," the woman who looked like Mrs. Santa Claus announced, and the MacDonald volunteers packed up their brochures for the night.

"Let's head back to the campsite," Mom said. "Nanag, you need to change out of your dance outfit so it's still fresh for tomorrow."

The thought of wading into the crowded campground was more than I could stomach. "I'll be along in a bit," I called.

Mom turned with a frown. "Tanya—"

"I want to grab some closing shots of the first day." I hitched the strap to the camcorder case back over my shoulder.

"Well . . . all right. We'll eat soon, though, so don't be too long."

Nodding, I headed out. On the lam. This video gig wasn't bad.

I wandered around the grounds for a while, but everyone really was packing up and shutting down, so there wasn't much to shoot. Finally I headed back through the parking field, dodging the mass exodus of suburban assault vehicles as day visitors headed home. But I stopped abruptly when I saw someone sitting on the ground by the scummy little pond.

Miguel. His pipes lay mute beside him. I hesitated, then started to back away. A twig snapped, though, and he turned and saw me. "Oh—Tanya."

"Hey. I didn't mean to disturb you. I just was, um, looking for some peace and quiet."

"Me too," Miguel said, but he gestured at the ground: an invitation to join him.

"I saw you with your grandmother," I said, settling down beside him. "Are you camping?"

"Yep. Right now she's playing canasta with some friends, though." Miguel grimaced mildly. "I told her I'd catch up later."

"I told my mom the same thing." With the sun setting, the air was growing cooler, and I leaned back on my hands and wiggled my toes appreciatively. I wore Birkenstock sandals, which were not in North Carolina vogue, but they made me feel at home. Lots of people in

Green Bay wear Birkies year-round. We do mostly put on socks when it gets really cold, though.

"It's chilly," Miguel said, in as gloomy a tone as I'd ever heard from him.

"Are you kidding? It's finally inching toward bearable."

He pointed at my shirt. "I figured you were just a Packers fan."

"Nope. I was born and raised in Green Bay."

"What's it like?"

How could I explain Wisconsin to someone from Puerto Rico? "Well . . . Wisconsin is beautiful, with lots of farms, and lots of lakes and forests, too. Green Bay is a small city in the northeast part. It's nice . . . except when the wind blows the wrong way and you can smell the paper factories."

"Doesn't it get awfully cold up there?"

"Well, it can get down to twenty or thirty below sometimes." I laughed at his expression. "But we get a lot of snow, too, and it has to be warmer than twenty below to snow."

"How can you live like that?" Miguel's expression suggested that the notion of any Homo sapiens existing voluntarily in Green Bay was beyond comprehension.

I shrugged. "It's whatever you're used to, I guess. We plug in our cars at night so they don't freeze, and make sure we have good snow tires, and dress in layers. The university where my mom used to work is built partially underground and all connected with tunnels."

He shook his head. "I'd like to see snow, but I don't think I could live there."

What Southern people don't understand is that living in a cold climate is not a sterile, icy experience. Coming into an air-conditioned house on a hot, muggy afternoon? That just feels . . . artificial. Stale. But there is no more wonderful feeling than coming indoors on a frigid day, to a fire on the hearth and warm cocoa and a bowl of home-made mushroom-barley soup. Days when sleet rattled the windows, or wind screamed around the eaves, gave me permission to curl up with a book when I got home from school. Cozy. Warm. Safe. There's nothing like that feeling in the South.

I sighed. "Well, mostly it's just . . . home, I guess. I lived there until last year. Never thought I'd end up in North Carolina."

"So how did you?"

"My parents got divorced." I was pleased with the even tone in my voice. "And my mom's parents were moving off their place and into an assisted-living apartment. So my mother decided to come back and move into their old house."

"Your mom is Scottish, right?"

"Well, she was just American until recently," I said. That came out sounding waspish, so I tried again. "Yes. She's a MacDonald."

He sat up straighter. "A MacDonald? Like Flora MacDonald?"

"Oh, please. Don't start on Saint Flora." I snapped a stick in two and tossed both bits at the pond. "Flora didn't mastermind the Bonnie Prince's escape after Culloden, you know. I had to read about it in school. She just did what she was asked to do. And did you know that during the Revolutionary War here, her husband raised Highland troops to fight *with* the British? And—"

"All *right* already," Miguel interrupted.

I felt my cheeks grow warm. "O.K. Sorry." I sighed. "I just get tired of hearing about it all. Mom's a librarian at the Scottish Heritage Center in Laurinburg. And she's a certified genealogical researcher. *And* she was just elected secretary of the local chapter of the Clan MacDonald Association." I didn't tell Miguel that I had learned early, after moving to North Carolina, that I had two choices: I could let Mom wax poetic and lengthy about all things Scottish, or I could complain and watch her withdraw, hurt and sad. And although that thick lavender bathrobe was no more, I could still see, beneath the tartan, glimpses of the woman who'd spent that day in front of the TV. No matter what, I didn't want to go back to that.

"What about you?" I asked. "Isn't it hard to leave Puerto Rico and come here?"

"Not really. I'm used to it. I've come every summer

since I was seven. My parents wanted me to get to know my relatives here."

"You must miss the ocean," I said. I was looking for some kind of common chord, and missing our place of origin seemed as likely as any.

But he shook his head again. "Here there are rivers and lakes. I'm going to be an aquatic botanist."

"Wouldn't you rather be an oceanographer?"

"No."

"But—why?" I wasn't trying to be rude, truly, but I just didn't get it. "I'd think that growing up on an island, at least mostly growing up there—"

"I like fresh water. It calls to me."

"Next you're going to tell me that it's in your genes."

"Maybe it is."

I stared at the pitiful little pond in front of us, so clogged with green slime that any self-respecting duck would take one look and keep flying. "If you want lakes, you should visit the Great Lakes. Lake Michigan, Lake Superior—they're awesome."

"I'd love to see them one day." For a moment he sounded wistful. "But there's plenty here to keep me busy."

"Doing what? Studying pond scum?"

He tossed me a disgusted look, then pointed at the pond. "Do you know what that green stuff is? *Lemna minor.* Duckweed. It may not look like much to you, but duckweeds are the smallest flowering plants on earth. I think that's pretty cool myself."

I stared at the green ooze. Somewhere behind me a car door slammed, and the sounds of a pipe band drifted in on the breeze. I suddenly felt very tired.

"Look, Miguel, I apologize," I muttered to my toes. "I don't know why I get so snotty sometimes."

He waved his hand. "It doesn't matter."

"Well . . . it does. But the point is, it doesn't have anything to do with *you*. You just happened to end up on the receiving end. And do *not* tell me it's because I'm a Highlander and you're a Lowlander," I added fiercely as he opened his mouth.

After a moment he said, "I don't think I could tell you anything."

I studied the spears of bright green grass poking up through last year's wheat-colored mat of dead stems. *Forward.* "Here's the thing," I heard myself say. "Lately I've developed this—this weird nasty streak."

"I could tell you were pissed about something earlier today," Miguel allowed.

Suddenly, it was a relief to confess my sins. "You don't know the half of it. When I went to my first dance competition—you know, where I screwed up—"

"Did you screw up? Really?" Miguel looked mildly pleased.

"You *know* I did. It was probably your fault!"

"*My* fault! What are you talking about?"

I regarded him with suspicion. "Are you trying to tell me that you don't remember what happened?"

"To you?" Miguel snorted. "I didn't even know you then. And I was keeping my eye on Mr. McCarthy. He's my bagpipes teacher, and he's got a lot of experience playing for dance competitions."

The heat in my cheeks began to fade. I was glad to know that my nightmare on stage wasn't tattooed permanently in Miguel's brain. "Well, there you go. I jump to bad conclusions, sometimes—"

"Yes, you do." He nodded solemnly.

"But the freakiest thing is with this girl, Christina. She's a dancer, and she's very nice, and I just *hate* her. I can't even say why. I just do."

"Oh." He considered. "My *abuelita* says—"

"Your what?"

"My other grandmother. In Puerto Rico. She says anger is often a mask for hurt feelings."

"But Christina's never *done* anything to me," I protested. "I'm telling you, I can't seem to get past it. All Christina Campbell has to do is walk by and—"

"Christina Campbell?" Miguel jerked his head in my direction. "Is that what you said?"

"Yeah? So?"

"Well, you're the one swimming in Scottish historical trivia, not me. Isn't there some kind of feud between the MacDonalds and the Campbells?"

"You mean about the Games or something?" I pictured the MacDonalds sulking because the Campbells won the Best Clan Tent award.

"No," Miguel said impatiently. "An ancient feud."

I suddenly remembered Nan reading that historical novel earlier and saying something about an old MacDonald feud. Maybe I should have paid more attention. "I think I read that most of the Campbells fought against Bonnie Prince Charlie and his Highlanders," I said, scraping my brain for tidbits from the Scottish History and Heritage course. "But I assure you, I don't give a rat's ass about it."

He shook his head. "It's not that. I'm sure I heard something somewhere about MacDonalds tangling with Campbells. And that would explain why you feel the way you do about Christina. Genetic mem—"

"I do *not* believe in genetic memory!"

He raised his eyebrows.

My hand actually *itched* to smack him. "Look, I better get going," I said, pushing to my feet. "My mom'll get mad if I hold up supper."

"O.K. I'll probably see you tomorrow."

"Yeah. Probably. See ya."

I hadn't taken more than a dozen steps before I heard bagpipe music scorch the air behind me: Miguel playing me off. It made me wonder if he didn't have a wee witchy streak of his own.

Chapter 9

The campground was crammed with campers, RVs, pop-ups, nylon pavilions, and a few plain old tents. The smell of frying hamburgers and hot dogs drifted through the early twilight. I wished mightily for the smell of bratwursts, which evidently are not as popular in North Carolina as they are in Wisconsin. I wouldn't have eaten any, but I wished I were somewhere where other people did.

But *that* thought reminded me of Dad, who grilled beer-boiled brats almost every weekend of the summer. He had not been supportive of my decision to become a vegetarian. "Eating meat is the natural order of things," he'd said the first time I presented him with a portobello mushroom cap I wanted grilled instead.

Well, here I was, hale and hearty and bratless.

The campground was carved in part from an old farm field and in part from a grove of pines. A lot of people had decorated their tiny slice of heaven with the ubiquitous tartan plaids. I passed several signs for family reunions and was absolutely delighted to see a sign labeled "Clan

MacRowdie" planted in the campsite just across the lane from our own.

I'm being sarcastic. There *is* no Clan MacRowdie. Not a real one, anyway. I heard singing and saw a bunch of people swigging ale and knew I was in for a long night.

Mom and Nan and I don't own a camper, so upon arrival we had fixed up our makeshift quarters with a family-sized tent from Sears, a few folding lawn chairs, a card table, and some cooking gear left over from my Girl Scout days. Mom now had two pots going over the fire, one of macaroni and cheese and one of ground beef, which the nonvegetarians among us (everyone but me) could mix together. Nan was busily stirring up a no-bake cheesecake.

"The cheesecake was supposed to be for tomorrow night!" I protested. "I had all the menus written out in the blue notebook. Didn't you check?"

Nan didn't look up. "You are such a control freak."

"You're just in time, Tanya," Mom said firmly, cutting that argument short. "Would you haul another jug of water for us? You know where the water buffalo is, right?"

I grabbed a couple of empty milk jugs and headed for the small tanker truck parked at the end of the row. I was trying to decide whether or not to ask Mom about the feud Miguel had mentioned—something between the MacDonalds and the Campbells—but just as I got back to our campsite, Doug MacDonald came by to double-check on the clan tent's volunteer schedule for the next day. He accepted my mother's invitation to stay for supper, which made me think he must have been planning to fix gruel for himself, for it wouldn't have taken much to beat our menu. Then a few more MacDonalds drifted by bearing mint brownies and taco chips and a bottle or two of Scotch, and somehow we ended up with a party that rivaled the MacRowdies' across the way. By the time things simmered down, we were all ready for bed.

By day, Nan has a delicate, elfin air about her. By night, she snores with a cadence resembling a snowplow driver trying to rev his engine at five degrees below zero. I, therefore, did not get a lot of sleep that night.

I think it is also, therefore, completely understandable that I was not at my best the next morning. "Tonight," I growled to my mother over a packet of instant oatmeal, "I will sleep in the car."

"Don't be ridiculous," Mom said. She stirred a cup of instant coffee with a fork.

"Mom, I cannot sleep with Nan snoring like a chain saw!"

"I do not snore!" Nan whimpered. This was not a new argument, and she was hypersensitive about the whole thing.

"Yes, you do! You kept the MacRowdies awake, and they were all drunk!"

"No more!" Mother held up a hand. "Tanya, we have one tent, and tonight we shall all sleep in it. Nanag, arguing about something that takes place while you're asleep is counterproductive. I don't want to hear another word about it."

Nan and I glared at each other. When Rosemary MacDonald came by with some rhubarb streusel coffeecake, and Nan and I crouched at campsite's edge to wash dishes, I hissed in Nan's ear, "You *do* snore."

She opened her mouth to spout yet another denial, then closed it again, eyes narrowing. I waited for whatever clever retort she was struggling to compose.

"Dad's coming down," she said.

She won that round.

Some bird shrilled in a tree overhead. A MacRowdie staggered from his campsite, which was otherwise still as a tomb. And from the distance came the wail of bagpipes. "What do you mean, Dad's coming down?" I finally managed.

"I asked him, and he said he would."

"When?"

"Last Wednesday—no, I guess it was Tuesday—"

I resisted the urge to wrap my soapy hands around her throat. "Not when did you call him, you idiot, when is he coming?"

"This weekend."

"He's coming *here?* To the Games?"

Nan nodded stubbornly. "I asked him to. I wanted him to see me dance."

For a moment I could hardly breathe. Finally I put the blue plastic bowl I was washing into the basin of dishwater and walked from the campsite. "Tanya?" Mom asked as I passed her and Rosemary. I croaked something about going for a walk.

I hadn't gotten far before I heard footsteps behind me. "Tanya, wait," Nan cried. The victory had fled from her voice. I ignored her. She grabbed my arm. *"Wait!"*

"Let go of me!" I jerked free and kept walking.

"Tanya!" she wailed again, but I was done talking. This time she didn't follow.

I passed a lot of other campsites filled with laughing people and shrieking kids. I smelled coffee and frying bacon. I almost got run down by a maniacal four-year-old on a Big Wheel. And I just kept walking.

Dad. Here. The thought brought that peculiar tight feeling to my chest.

When Mom and Dad split up, it came as a shock to Nan and me. I hadn't seen it coming, even though Dad spent more time with his new actor friends than with us. Hadn't thought to worry, even though half of my friends had divorced parents. Mom and Dad each tried to talk to us about it, but neither said much beyond "sometimes things happen" and "growing apart." I think Dad even said something about "irreconcilable differences." And for a while I believed that.

But I found out exactly what those irreconcilable differences were.

It happened on Halloween night, a few weeks after Dad moved out. A friend of Nan's named Ashley had arrived to trick-or-treat with Nan and then spend the night. Ashley ate one too many candy bars and threw up on the Oriental carpet in the living room. Ashley's parents were out of town, so Mom put her to bed in Nan's room and doubled Nan and me in mine. When I couldn't lie in bed and listen to Nan snore for one more minute, I slipped outside.

I was planning to go downstairs and read, but I heard voices. Mom and Dad. I crept to the head of the stairs. I could just see a corner of that Oriental rug, splotchy-damp from where Mom had cleaned it. Mom and Dad were arguing in hushed, bitter tones. Then Mom spit out some words like bullets: "For God's sake, Jim. I *saw* you two. In my own house. In my own bedroom."

Something started buzzing in my ears. My skin tingled. I slid to the floor in a silent, numb heap.

When I could finally hear again, Mom was saying, "How long would this have gone on if I hadn't forgotten my checkbook that day?"

Dad kept murmuring things like, "No, no, it was just the once, I *swear* it," and "I never meant to hurt you," and "This has been hard on me, too."

That last one just about did Mom in. "Hard on *you?*" she screeched.

"Don't wake the girls," Dad said—ordered, actually. "I don't want them to know I came over tonight."

Like Mom or I cared what he wanted.

What I wanted was to will myself back in time. Back to when my parents simply had "irreconcilable differences" like 52.7 percent of all couples in the United States.

I had lain in the darkness of the purple bedroom I'd grown up in, listening to Nan snore and the Manellis' wiener dog yapping at its shadow next-door. A little while later I'd heard a car start in front of the house and saw the flash of headlights as my father pulled away.

A year and a half later, it felt just as raw to relive it again. Breathe, I told myself, and forced my hands to un-clench. I could almost hear Mom saying, *Let it out, Tanya.* That hard, tight feeling was still lodged beneath my ribs, and I *wanted* to cry. But nothing came. I tried to kick a rock, but my sandal came off and I had to hobble into the underbrush to retrieve it. Birkies aren't the best footgear for kicking things.

I left the campground behind and stalked toward the festival grounds. The official activities didn't begin for an-other hour, but some of the athletes were warming up for the Heavies on the main field. I saw a beefy man with a shaved head and walrus mustache pick up a "hammer"—

an iron ball on a four-foot handle. He swung it over his head three times, then hurled it down the field.

I wanted to hurl one, too. I wanted to *fling* one, with all my might. I wanted to do damage.

I approached him. "Excuse me . . . may I see that?"

"Hunh?" The athlete blinked at me, obviously not used to teenaged girls interrupting his morning practice.

"I'm doing some research," I hedged, looking covetously at the large hammer dangling from his hand. "For the student projects competition."

He shrugged, and I curled my fingers around the handle. It was heavier than I expected, and I almost dropped it on my toes. I needed a moment to get a firm grasp on the thing. Then I swung my arm back and let fly.

"*Heads up!*" the hammer's rightful owner bellowed in horror.

Let me be clear: the hammer didn't really come *that* close to hitting anyone, although I will admit that the projectile did not sail as straight and true as I had hoped. Nor as far. And since I just about wrenched my arm out of its socket, I think I suffered more damage than anyone. I didn't even feel better.

I guess a girl whose best sport involves standing in the outfield praying that no one hits a ball her way isn't destined to vent her ire in the Heavies. So I sat on the bleachers stewing. I needed to either chill out or lie low when Dad arrived, or he might just find himself at the wrong end of a hammer throw. One way or another.

I had tried to tell Mom, just before we left Green Bay, that I *knew*. About Dad. We were sitting on the floor, me making lists on index cards—yellow, for kitchen stuff—to tape on the moving boxes. Mom was emptying drawers. "Drat *everything!*" she flared, out of nowhere, and threw a spoon across the kitchen. I froze, my heart banging as if she'd thrown it at me. "I can't find the spatula!" she quavered, and her eyes brimmed over.

"Mom," I said after a long moment. "I know. About Dad, I mean."

Mom wiped her eyes real quick. "Oh, here it is, under the pie pans," she said in a too-bright voice. So I'd backed off. And in all the months since then, we'd both acted as if I'd never said it. I sometimes wondered if Mom had truly talked herself into believing that I didn't know the truth.

I didn't have that luxury.

And Nan? There had been many times I wanted to tell her. Like when she sobbed herself to sleep after Dad canceled his first flight to North Carolina to see us in January—something about a blizzard; and his second flight in March, with no real explanation. Like when she accuses me of hurting his feelings. Like when she criticizes me for not calling him. And like when she does incredibly *stupid* things like inviting him to the Cross

Creek Highland Games. There are times when I want to fling what I know in her face like a handful of mud.

But then I look into her thin face. She's as trusting as a puppy, and just as vulnerable. So I never do.

I drummed my heels against the bleachers. Dad would probably cancel out this time, too. I hoped he would . . . but then Nan's weekend would be ruined, and Mom and I would have a weepy twelve-year-old on our hands. One way or another, this most sucky weekend was about to get worse.

Chapter 10

When I figured Mom and Nan were gone—Mom to the MacDonald clan tent and Nan off to the dance arena—I went back to the campsite to pick up the camcorder. My anger about Dad had faded into something straddling fatigue and depression. I needed to lose myself in my work.

Mom and Nan and I had visited a few Highland Games last summer, when we were still new to the whole Scottish immersion thing. Mom mostly wanted to hang at the clan tents, and Nan mostly wanted to hang at the dance stage, but we did watch some of the athletic competitions. And they corked me off. While the men hurled a variety of extremely heavy objects extremely far distances, women competed in the broomstick toss and frying pan toss and haggis hurl. I am not making that up. And, oh yes, once I truly saw a "bonniest knees" competition taking place. This male domination, based no doubt on traditions of the great Highland warrior, would make a good theme within my documentary.

Back at the main field, I shot some B-Roll of the athletes warming up. I also found several athletes who agreed to an interview. Wearing T-shirts and athletic shoes and, of course, kilts, they stood around drinking some kind of blue sports drink and looking masculine.

"Ready?" I squinted through the monitor at the first subject, a bulky college student named Charles who appeared capable of flattening Arnold Schwarzenegger with one hand. "O.K. Why do you participate in the athletic competitions?"

Charles considered. "Well, because it's fun, and—"

"Sorry," I interrupted him, belatedly remembering the first rule the WPNE producers had taught me about interviewing. "Could you repeat the question in your answer?"

Charles ran a hand through his brown curls. I suspected he was gaining a new appreciation of the complexities of making documentaries. "I participate in the heavy athletic competitions because it's fun," he said dutifully. "There's a lot of camaraderie."

I lined up his buddy Glen next. "Why do you participate, Glen?" I asked, trying to hold the camera steady. I wished I had a tripod.

"Well, pretty much what he said." Glen jerked his head toward Charles. I remembered the second rule: separate your subjects.

Time to move on to the serious stuff, anyway. I shifted

focus to the third man. Randy was, I learned, a drywall installer from Phoenix who'd flown in to compete at these games. He was taller and leaner than the other two and wore his blue-and-black kilt and black tank top with an easy grace a girl could grow used to. Anyone who thinks that real men don't wear skirts should come to a heavy event.

"O.K., Randy. Part of what I'm doing is exploring the myths that have grown up around Highland Games. The first Highland Games was held in the 1950s. I know they've been growing ever since, but do you think these events command the same respect as regular track-and-field events, which have existed since ancient times?"

"Actually," Randy said politely, "as I understand it, the first Games held in this country took place in 1835 or 1836. Somewhere in there. In New York, I think."

Third rule: always interview a subject *off*-camera first so you don't waste tape on surprises.

"Highland Games were the first organized track-and-field events to appear in North America," Randy continued. "They didn't really get going until after the American Civil War, though."

"Are you sure?" I couldn't help asking. This just didn't sound right to me. I'd heard the local Scots discussing, with enormous pride, the inception of Highland Games. And they weren't talking about the nineteenth century.

"Yeah, I am sure. You're probably thinking of the first

Highland Games in North Carolina. You're right about that. Grandfather Mountain, 1956."

"But still, they're an American manifestation," I persisted. "People of Scottish descent have created them to—"

"Actually, I think they go back to ancient Scotland." Randy rubbed his palms together, warming to his subject. "Heavy athletic competitions were sponsored by kings and chiefs so they could choose the strongest men as bodyguards. Last year I talked to some guy who was doing his dissertation on Highland Games, and he said that happened as early as the sixth century."

Frankly, this interview wasn't my best. Ethical question: should I broaden the focus of my documentary or simply keep looking until I found material that supported my thesis? Despite this minor comeuppance, my belief in my basic premise—that the so-called heritage embraced at Highland Games is largely a wistful invention—remained unshaken.

As I thanked the men, Charles gave me a tip: "You should check out the women athletes, too."

I snorted. "Tossing a frying pan?"

"No, tossing a caber," Glen said calmly.

"A *caber?*" I believe my jaw dangled. A caber is a pine tree with its limbs axed off, about the size of a telephone pole. The athletes pick it up so it's standing upright in their hands, run a few feet, and hurl it end over end. No lie.

Charles grinned. These guys were having way too much fun playing stump-the-documentarian. "There are some serious women athletes, you know. They've been on the circuit for a few years, and this year the Cross Creek Games opened up women's categories."

"Where are they?" Scanning the field, I didn't see anything but men.

"Field B."

After I thanked him and they headed back to the field, I realized I hadn't gotten their written consent to use the interviews—absolutely the most important step in the process—but decided that the risk of lawsuit was minimal. I wasn't in the mood to go running after these guys.

People were beginning to wander toward the bleachers. The second day of the Cross Creek Highland Games was officially underway. I was trying to figure out where Field B was when a blare like a gut-shot moose screeched in my ear. Whirling, I saw Miguel, neatly kilted, his cursed bagpipes tucked under his arm. I glowered. He grinned.

"That is not amusing," I observed.

"I've been looking all over for you. I've got practice soon, and our pipe band's first round of competition is at eleven, and—" He must have read something in my expression, because he ended that recitation abruptly. "Want to have a picnic later?"

This surprise invitation, on top of the women/caber

thing, left me too jangled to come up with a gracious response. "Um, I guess so. But no pipes!"

"Noon? I'll meet you at the pond."

"O.K., but—," I began, but he was already on his way. Guys. Who could figure them out?

I'd had a boyfriend in Green Bay. Well, sort of. Stephen Hoobler. He sat behind me in World History. We got assigned to the same small group research project about the origins of World War I, and one girl didn't do anything and one got mono and was out sick for pretty much the whole time, so Stephen and I ended up doing all the work. He was a solid C plus student and volunteered at the local Boys & Girls Club, which I thought was interesting because philanthropy is definitely not the cool thing by most kids' standards.

We went to a couple of basketball games together, and once to a movie, and sometimes hung out at each other's houses. Stephen always kissed me good-night, although he never tried to do anything else, and I wasn't sure what to make of that. When I found out I was moving to North Carolina, Stephen and I went to Bay Beach Wildlife Sanctuary one Saturday afternoon and sat on a bench watching some Canada geese swimming back and forth, and talked about trying to stay in touch. But I could tell that his heart wasn't in it. We e-mailed a few times and talked once on the phone. That was pretty much the extent of my experience with boys.

Well, I was up for a picnic with Miguel. I checked my watch—plenty of time to get more taping in before the rendezvous at Duckweed Pond. After a half-hour of searching, I found Field B, which turned out to be a muddy bit of turf behind a wall of porta-potties, bordered by a single row of benches. And I found one lone woman athlete, a tall blond who exuded magnificent strength without looking hulking. I watched her hurl a *clachneart* (which is sort of like a shot put) a few times and concluded that she was descended from Amazon warrior women, or Vikings, or possibly Xena the Warrior Princess.

I waited until she took a much-deserved juice break before humbly approaching and introducing myself. "Sheila Silber," she said. When I explained that I was making a documentary, she grinned. "Sure, you can interview me. Want a bran muffin?"

I declined the muffin, and we settled on one of the benches. For the time being, I left the camcorder in its case and relied on notebook and pen instead. "I must confess," I began, needing absolution, "that until this morning I didn't even know there *were* women athletes at Highland Games."

"Some of the Games still don't have women's competitions," Sheila said. "When I got started, I had to compete against the men. Most of 'em didn't like that, but I qualified fair and square. So some of the committees started letting us in."

"That's amazing," I said, remembering the feel of the hammer I'd barely been able to lift, much less hurl.

"I wouldn't say we've made it yet," Sheila added wryly, and gestured toward her arena. "The men get the main field and grandstand. The women get mud and a row of porta-johns. But things are getting better."

Sheila explained that she had competed in track-and-field events in college, and a friend introduced her to Highland Games.

"Are you Scottish?" I asked.

She grinned again. "I'm a mutt."

This was more like what I was looking for. "Do you mind if I turn on the camera now?" I asked, whipping out the camcorder. Clouds were skittering over the sun, so the light was problematic, but I didn't want to lose the moment. "O.K. Could you tell me that again?"

Looking amused, she shook her head, making her blond ponytail whip back and forth. "I'm a mutt," she repeated. "From what my folks tell me, my lines have been on this continent for generations. We seem to have a little bit of lots of things—German, Irish, Italian, Swedish."

I tried to remember where the Vikings originated, then realized Sheila was waiting for the next question. "Since you're not Scottish, why do you participate in these Games?"

She considered, chewing her muffin thoughtfully.

"Well, in regular track-and-field events, it's just athletics. I mean, people work really hard and everything—I sure did—but that's all there is. At the Highland Games, there's the music, and the dancing, and all the culture . . . it's a much richer experience."

As if on cue, somewhere in the distance a pipe and drum band let loose. I felt the first hint of a headache pinch deep in my skull. "But if you're not Scottish . . ."

"It's not my culture, you mean?" Sheila laughed. "Who cares? I'll tell you, the first time I went to a Highland Games and saw the Betty Crocker events—"

"You mean the rolling pin toss?" I couldn't help smiling.

"You got it. It made me mad. The first event I officially participated in, the rolling pin toss was all I could enter. So I tossed it almost a hundred feet."

"No way!"

"I used to be pretty good at the discus," Sheila said modestly. "I used the same technique. Anyway, then I went over to the men's field and found out the qualifying distances and bettered 'em."

I would have nodded in satisfaction if I hadn't been holding the camera.

Sheila folded her napkin and stuffed it into a tiny cooler. "There are a lot of really amazing women athletes getting involved in Highland Games. And what I really like is how that reflects on Scottish women."

I was definitely behind the curve this morning. "Um, could you elaborate on that?"

"It just seems like women always have to carry the heaviest burden." She took a sip of orange juice. "Sometimes I think this Highland heritage stuff focuses too much on the men."

I decided she was on to something.

"It's the whole Highland warrior thing." Sheila shrugged. "Hey, I'm no expert. But I've read some stuff since I got started in all of this. From what I can tell, Scottish women historically were kick-ass tough. In my own way, I like to remind people how incredible—hey, Gail! I haven't seen you since the Sacramento Games!"

The interview ended abruptly as Sheila leapt up to embrace another athlete. I promised to come back later, when the actual competitions began, and took my leave.

Scottish women, kick-ass tough. Really? If that was true, why didn't I see and hear more about it at the Highland Games? You'd think the only Scottish woman worth a crumb of shortbread was Flora MacDonald—she who supposedly saved Bonnie Prince C.'s royal butt after the battle of Culloden.

The role of Scottish women in history had little to do with the scope of my documentary. Still . . . I had to admit, I was curious.

Chapter 11

I looked at my watch again, thought about Mom and Nan, and figured I owed both of them an appearance.

At the dance venue, visitors packed the wooden benches fronting the stage. Veteran dance parents had staked claims on the side areas and settled in with lawn chairs, coolers, awnings, and bags packed with extra hair gel and emergency sewing kits and energy bars. I couldn't blame Nan for wanting someone, *someone,* to be there for her. She deserved a granola bar or two, and a proud parent parked in a chaise lounge with a can of ginger ale and plenty of sunscreen.

The about-to-compete waited in a cordoned-off space near the stage. I saw my sister warming up for her round in the *Seann Triubhas* (that's "shawn trews"), which translates to "old trousers." Miss Janet once explained that the dance supposedly harks back to 1746, when the English banned the wearing of plaids in Scotland after the battle of Culloden—all part of their plan to destroy Highland culture. The *Seann Triubhas* represents the Scots kicking off the despised, English-imposed trousers.

I wasn't in the mood to talk dancing with anyone and kept my shoulders hunched against the possible vision of Christina Campbell, Goddess of Highland Dancing. But I hovered until I caught Nan's eye and gave her a thumbs-up. A tentative, grateful smile lit her face. Then I squeezed into a child-sized spot in front of the stage and sat through at least three dozen rounds of the stupid dance —accompanied by bagpipes, of course—and got her whole performance on videotape—wide shots, closeups, and a couple of masterful zooms, if I do say so myself. When the dance concluded, I stood up, clapping wildly. "Woo-hoo!" I yelled. "Go, Nan!" I saw Nan blush and smile, and thought that maybe I wasn't entirely worthless after all.

Then I cut back to clan row, where I found Mom at the genealogy table. A couple of visitors were leafing through fat notebooks, looking up countless litters of MacDonalds, but a gray-haired gentleman had taken a seat across from Mom. "Genealogy isn't for the fainthearted," Mom was saying, leaning forward intently. "You have to make a commitment. And you might as well forget the whole thing if you're worried about what you might discover. Thieves, scoundrels, rogues—sometimes they're the easiest to find, because they leave more of a paper trail."

The man allowed that while he wasn't afraid of a few skeletons in his closet, he didn't have much time to go digging himself, and then Mom allowed that while she'd give him any advice she could, perhaps he should take one of her cards in case he decided to have a certified professional genealogist do the legwork.

When Mom noticed me waiting, she asked that Mrs. Santa Claus lady to take her spot for a while. "Tanya, I was worried about you," she scolded without preamble. "You left the campsite so abruptly this morning. . . ."

We headed around the tent to the private area behind. "Mom, Nan told me she invited Dad to come down. And that he's actually *coming.*"

Two round spots of color suddenly stained Mom's cheeks, but she only nodded her head. "Yes, she told me, too."

"Do you know when?"

"Sometime this afternoon, I think."

"I'm really sorry, Mom."

She pinched her lips together for a few seconds, then took a deep breath. "Tanya, what happened between your father and me is in the past. I can handle seeing him from time to time. I'm fine. *Truly.* I don't want you to worry for my sake."

It occurred to me that maybe my mom was the kind of kick-ass tough lady Sheila was talking about.

"This is very important for Nan," Mom was saying. "Doug promised to relieve me here this afternoon so I can go see her dance the reel, but the truth is, I'm not being as supportive of her efforts this weekend as I would like."

"You have a right to have fun, too, Mom. You've earned it."

"What I need to keep earning is a living," she said quietly. "And staying at the tent here is one of the best ways for me to meet potential clients."

I wondered suddenly if Dad was behind on child support or something. Mom never talked about stuff like that. "Well, I just videotaped Nan's entire performance of the *Seann Triubhas*," I told her, and was rewarded by a flood of gratitude in her eyes.

"Thank you, dear." She cocked her head. "Now, what about you? Are you going to be all right with your father here?"

"Sure, Mom."

She regarded me. "Liar."

"Mom! Stop. I'm fine."

"All right," she said in that tone mothers use when they want you to know that they're backing off only out of kindness. "But, hey—wouldn't you like to wear a MacDonald sash today?"

"Not really." She never quits. I let her kiss my forehead, and then she went back to work.

I spent the rest of the morning shooting some of the men's athletic events. Since there were fewer female participants, their events didn't officially start until afternoon. The Cross Creek Games organizers had also added a children's round. A delighted little girl wearing a crown of streaming ribbons and sparklies won the sheaf toss. It involved a small straw-filled burlap bag and a kid-sized plastic snow shovel.

By eleven-thirty my stomach was telling me that my breakfast bowl of instant oatmeal, although vaguely Scottish, was long gone. I suspect the ancient lairds and warriors relied on a heartier variety. Miguel hadn't said who was supposed to bring food for our picnic, so I figured I better play it safe and pick something up. I scoped out the food tents and ended up with veggie haggis. It was the only entrée without meat and seemed to be selling pretty well. I guess a lot of people who want to try haggis aren't up to the real thing.

When I reached the pond, Miguel wasn't in sight. I put the food sack and the camera bag down and sighed. Scenic this spot was not, but at least it was quiet.

After a moment I wandered down to the edge of the pond. The green scum sat on the water like skin on pudding. Crouching, I looked closer. Suppressing a grimace, I dipped a tentative finger into the slime.

It didn't feel slimy, actually. My finger emerged with a

few traces of bright lime green on the skin. I stared at it, inches from my nose, and saw minuscule round leaves.

Pond scum, I'd called it. Duckweed, Miguel had called it. One of the smallest flowering plants on earth. He thought it was special—

"Hey," someone said over my shoulder, and I just about immersed myself in all that duckweed. When I regained my balance, I turned to Miguel. "Don't sneak up on me like that!"

"*Mac gun Athair.*"

I groaned. "Gaelic. What did that mean, hello or something?"

"No. *Mac gun Athair* is the Gaelic name for *Lemna minor.* Duckweed."

"You have *got* to be kidding me."

He grinned in that annoying way he had. "Nope, it's true. I'm just learning, taking a beginner's course, and thought it would be more fun if I learned some words that had meaning for me. I gave my instructor a list. I think the botanical names about did him in, but he came through. He had to send to Scotland for some of them."

"You are out of your mind."

"'The green mantle of the standing pool.' That's from *King Lear.* I'm pretty sure Shakespeare was thinking about duckweed when he wrote that."

"Do you spend all of your time on arcane pursuits?"

Miguel looked stung. "It's not arcane. Duckweeds can absorb excess nutrients from surface waters. They have tremendous potential in wastewater treatment."

I simply did not know what to say.

"I brought lunch," Miguel said brightly, and I allowed myself to be led a safe distance from the brink.

"I brought food, too," I told him. "You didn't tell me who was buying."

"That's O.K. We'll share."

I did most of the sharing, since he'd brought two meat-filled shepherd's pies. For such a skinny kid, he sure packed it away. Maybe bagpiping burns a lot of calories.

"Hey," he said abruptly, after wolfing down most of his lunch. "Have you thought any more about the idea of genetic memory?"

"No!"

He held up his hands, palms out. "O.K.! But can I ask you a question?"

"I suppose," I said, instantly suspicious.

"Did your house in Green Bay have a fireplace?"

I don't know what I'd been expecting, but that wasn't it. "Yeah. Why?"

"We don't have a fireplace at home in Puerto Rico," he said mildly. "And my grandma's apartment doesn't have one, either. I was just wondering what it's like to have a fire indoors."

I forked up some haggis. "Well, it's nice. Especially when it's really cold, or during an ice storm or something."

"But you had central heating, too, right?"

"Yeah."

"So you didn't make fires in your fireplace just to get warm?"

"What is up with you?" I snapped. "Of course not. It's just . . . I don't know, cozy or something to have a fire."

He leaned back on his elbows, grinning.

"*What?*" I demanded. "You are plucking on my very last nerve."

"And *you* have just illustrated one of the most common examples of genetic memory. Why do people have indoor fireplaces, even though they have central heat? Why do people love campfires, even in the summer? What is it about staring at flames that people find so compelling?"

I pinched my lips together, trying to find a retort.

"I believe it's genetic," he finished. "To prehistoric people, fire represented everything: safety, warmth, light. Every human being on earth today is descended from some band of those first people, so we all share that instinctive urge to gather around a fire. We're plugging into something very primal, encoded in our genes."

"That's quite a theory," I said feebly, struggling to wrap my brain around what he'd said.

"O.K., I'm done now." He sat back up. "How's your documentary coming along?"

Glad to move on, I told him about my morning.

"Oh, I love watching the Heavies," Miguel said. "I'll have to check the schedule. Maybe I can watch some this afternoon."

I took another bite of soy haggis. It was spicy and filling, not bad at all. "Some of the athletes were interesting to talk to," I admitted. "Especially that woman. But the guys were telling me stuff about the ancient origins of the athletic events—I'm not sure about all that. It sounded sorta contrived to me."

Miguel rolled his eyes. "Why can't you just let things be?"

"Because . . . people want to know, that's why. I want to know what's real and what's not. Documentaries have to show the truth—"

"But why is your truth *the* truth?"

I paused. Opened my mouth, closed it again. Finally I managed, "I don't know what you mean."

"Well, it bugs you that we all wear kilts, right? Because they evolved from a form of dress that only the Highlanders wore?"

"That's right. Historically, Lowlanders didn't wear plaids. And the kilts we wear today didn't emerge until Victorian—"

"I don't care!" Miguel interrupted. "Just listen for once. At some point in history, even the Highlanders didn't wear plaids. They ran around in furs or something. It seems to me that you've picked a certain period in history to pin all your assumptions of truth around—"

"*My* assumptions of truth—"

"People here celebrating their Scottish heritage have done the same thing," Miguel pressed on, with the determination of a Border collie on patrol. "They've just picked a different date. Or *dates,* maybe. But anyway, why are you right, and the rest of us wrong?"

I chewed slowly, constructing my answer. "Any documentary comes through the lens, if you will, of its creator. So I have to show things as I . . ." My voice trailed away when I realized I was adding more fuel to his fire, not mine. "Well, Sheila isn't even Scottish," I finally added, feeling uncomfortably disloyal to one of the nicest people I'd met all weekend. "And she says one of the things she likes about participating at Highland Games is the culture. Doesn't that strike you as even a little bit odd?"

Miguel fumbled in his sporran, that little leather purse-type thing guys wear with their kilts, and pulled out a couple of napkins. "No," he said, offering one to me. "She may have Scottish blood she's not even aware of—"

"*Oh puh-leez!*"

"Or maybe she just wishes she did." Miguel grinned

at me again. "Is that shortbread? I didn't think to bring dessert."

It annoyed me to realize that our debate had annoyed me much more than Miguel. I let him eat most of the shortbread and absently agreed to meet him at the grandstand in time to watch the caber competition. He polished off a bottle of root beer and then trotted off, back to his next performance or rehearsal or whatever. Back to the other musicians in his band, who had evidently opened their arms to this Puerto Rican transplant who had opened his arms to them.

Miguel was a nice guy, even if he didn't shy from an argument. I could tell he didn't intend anything mean by his observations. But he didn't realize that when he chipped away at my belief in my abilities as a documentarian, he was chipping at the only thing I had left to stand on.

I sat for a long time, staring at that green mantle *King Lear* spoke of.

Pond scum.

Chapter 12

Grandpa Zeshonski used to say, "If life gives you scraps, make sausage." I didn't think that stuffing the scraps into a sack made of intestines did much to improve things, but I never said so. I adored Grandpa Zeshonski, even though spending the after-school hours of my formative years in a butcher shop probably had a lot to do with my ultimate decision to go veggie. But I didn't renounce meat until after he died. I just didn't have it in me.

Anyway, Grandpa Z. was a wise old guy. He was the real thing, born in Poland, who wore his ancestry like a comfortable old sweater. When Nan and I were little, he and Gramma sometimes took us to taverns—it's sort of a family thing in Wisconsin, although not, I've learned, in the Bible Belt—and we'd play cards and eat fried perch on Friday nights, and sometimes a polka band would play and everybody, little kids and old people and everyone in between, would dance. And on Sundays we'd go to Mass, and Grandpa would mutter prayers in Polish, and we'd go home and eat the stuffed pasta pockets called *pierogies* and the stuffed cabbage rolls called *golabki.* And see, that never felt forced or artificial. It just was.

Well, scraps was about all I was ending up with this weekend. I didn't know if I could salvage my documentary. But I could at least try to stuff all that raw footage into a sack of intestines, figuratively speaking, and see if I could find a halfway decent bratwurst along the way.

First, though, I decided to check on Nan and make sure the poor kid had gotten some lunch, so I swerved back to the dance arena. The area was blessedly quiet, the stage empty. Dancers were sprawled ungracefully in lawn chairs, sipping iced tea and eating sandwiches provided by doting parents.

I scanned the crowd and was just about to give up when I spotted Nan at one of the more involved family setups. In the shade of a blue awning, Mr. Campbell relaxed in a chaise lounge—the kind with drink holders built right into the armrest—while Mrs. Campbell spread a bountiful lunch on a folding table. Nan stood like a lady-in-waiting, watching Christina Campbell spritz her already perfect hair.

My heart began to beat too fast. I found myself marching toward Camp Campbell.

"It really wouldn't be any trouble, Nanag," Mrs. Campbell said as I approached. "One of the benefits of working as a school guidance counselor is being free in the summer. I wouldn't mind picking you up—"

"Hello," I called, trying *really* hard to make my voice sound natural.

Nan scrambled to meet me, awkward because she'd pulled rubber rain boots over her ghillies to keep them from getting scuffed. Her expression was half pleased and half wary. "Hey, Tanya. Guess what? Christina goes to a special dance clinic every other week when school's out. And Mrs. Campbell said she can drive if I want to go!"

Christina eyed me as she selected a celery stick from the buffet. She ate the whole thing before saying, "You could come with us."

"I'll be working this summer," I said. "I need to make money."

"Christina's got a job, too," Mr. Campbell said. "She's going to be interning at the Chamber of Commerce. But she got permission to leave early on those Wednesdays."

"I'll have to pass," I said. With my luck I'd probably end up flipping burgers that summer and doubted I'd be able to arrange special hours—even if I wanted to. "Nan, I just came to see if you'd eaten."

"Mom gave me some tuna salad." Nan pointed to a bowl on the table. "And Christina invited me to eat here."

Mrs. Campbell began passing out paper plates, all tucked into wicker holders so they couldn't collapse. "Would you like to join us for lunch, Tanya?" Her tone was polite.

"No, thank you. I've already eaten." I nodded at my sister. "See you later, Nan."

I hadn't gotten far before I heard someone call my name. I turned and saw Christina Campbell coming after me. She wore snug booties over *her* ghillies, hand-knit in a shade that exactly matched her kilt. When she caught up with me, she kept her voice low. "Look, is something going on?"

"Going on?" I repeated, wondering who I could get to teach me to knit.

She frowned impatiently. "Did I tick you off or something? 'Cause if I did, I sure don't know how."

"No, I just—that is . . ." I took a deep breath. "I'm just trying to figure out why someone your age wants to hang out with Nan."

Christina folded her arms over her chest. "I often help the younger girls, and Nanag is sweet. I like teaching."

This goes *way* beyond teaching, I wanted to say. Nan already has a dance teacher. And she already has a big sister and a mom!

But I couldn't spit the words out. Nan didn't start dancing as young as most of the girls she was competing against, and she needed any boost she could get. In the old days Dad had driven me and Nan to the pool or church activities or whatever in the summer, but those days were gone. Mom couldn't drive Nan to dance clinics during the day, and I didn't have my license yet.

"I appreciate it," I finally said.

"Fine, then."

"Fine."

We each turned around and marched away. But before getting swept up in the crowd on the main path, I turned back. I could see Nan munching a sandwich, chattering between bites. Christina said something, and her father laughed. *Good one, Sunshine!* I imagined him saying.

Out of nowhere a flashback of that nightmarish audition for *Annie* two years earlier began to replay in my head. I remembered the look in my father's eyes when I'd finally stumbled offstage. I remembered Nan's expression, too. I'd seen it again when I screwed up the wretched sword dance.

I pulled my camcorder from the bag, let it settle against my palm, and felt my blood pressure begin to slide back toward normal. I needed to get to work.

On the festival grounds I decided to scope out vendor row, where visitors could buy "Up Your Kilt" T-shirts, tartan pajamas, CDs of pipe band music, "You CAN Speak Gaelic" courses on cassette, and clan badges on bumper stickers, shot glasses, golf hats, etc., etc. The tents were packed, and I shot a minute or two of the crowd scene, but I was looking for something else.

I almost missed it. A sign for The Proud Thistle didn't exactly call my name—I'd spent too many hours digging proud thistles out of our backyard to feel much affinity for Scotland's national emblem. And unlike most of the vendors, who had rolled up their canvas walls to help accommodate traffic and allow for a breeze, this proprietor allowed fresh air and visitors to enter only through a front opening.

After I ducked inside and my eyes adjusted, I understood the precaution. The Proud Thistle sold old prints and maps and used books. Not the beat-up, twenty-five-cent variety. Some of these looked *old.* Definitely not the kind of thing to leave sitting in the sun.

I flipped through the bins of prints first and found several I thought would work well for the documentary: a classic 1845 print of a MacLachlan warrior, looking menacing; a reproduction of a painting of Flora MacDonald, looking virtuous and maidenly; a map of Scotland, showing original locations of all the clans, including the Lowlanders.

I also found a page featuring several drawings of men competing at a Highland Games. It was from an old *Harper's Weekly,* dated July 10, 1867. Well. It seemed this whole Highland Games thing *had* been going on for quite some time.

The print featured one woodcut of a man in full costume—excuse me, national dress—about to hurl a stone, and another of a man hurling a hammer. At the bottom were sketches of grown men engaged in wheelbarrow and sack races, looking ridiculous. At the top a man danced a Highland fling for the judges while a piper piped. And the biggest sketch, in the center, showed five men identified as "Resident Chiefs." There wasn't a woman in sight on the entire page. Evidently the whole affair was *totally* a guy thing in 1867. Way to go, Sheila.

When I told the man with the cashbox about my documentary, he gave me permission to roll up one tent flap and put the prints I had selected on a table in the sun long enough to get a quick shot. Each print was sandwiched between cardboard and a piece of plastic wrap, the latter being firmly sealed, and I realized belatedly that the chances of getting a decent image through plastic were slim. Plastic reflects light. Plus, I didn't have a tripod. This situation really demanded careful lighting and no plastic and a lock-down shot, as the WPNE videographer used to call it.

At that moment I was ready to believe that I had no future in the world of documentaries. But I didn't want to admit that to the owner, so I did my best.

Once the prints were all shot and safely back in their bins, I took a quick turn around the shelves and tables of books. There were scads of clan histories, and the required volumes devoted to the Culloden massacre. Some of the very old books, neatly encased in protective Mylar jackets, covered Scottish history and culture. Those I passed by. But a shelf of used paperbacks squatted in one corner, none looking too old or valuable. And the title on one of the spines just jumped out at me.

When I blinked and doubled back, I realized the offensive words were truly part of the title: *Damn' Rebel*

Bitches: The Women of the '45. I pulled the book from the shelf. The contents page listed chapters like "Warrior Maidens" and "The Monstrous Regiment of Women." Flora MacDonald rated only one slim chapter, and that didn't start until page 111.

What the heck! The bookseller had done me a favor. I should repay his kindness. I bought the book.

Once it was safely squeezed into the camera bag, I headed toward the door. I almost made it, but something else snagged my attention—a coffee-table book about Scottish castles. I'm not the sort to get poetic about Scottish castles, but I figured I could probably use a classic shot or two for my film. I paused to flip through the book. The images were predictable: heathered hills, scenic castles, blah blah blah. The final section was labeled "Haunted Castles." Ah, ghost stories! A mainstay of Scottish folklore.

I was chuckling out loud when my hand stilled on a page. All at once—I swear this is true—the temperature in the tent seemed to drop forty degrees or so. My gaze locked on the photo before me.

"Dunstaffnage Castle, on the west coast of Scotland," the caption read. I'd never heard of it before and couldn't imagine what was creeping me out. Granted, this was no Disneyland castle of fairy tale turrets and spires. Dunstaffnage Castle was a forbidding-looking thing, square, built at cliff's edge with a straight plunge down to the sea. Still . . .

Descriptive text began below the photo: "Flora MacDonald, Bonnie Prince Charlie's heroine, was briefly held prisoner in this castle in 1746. . . ."

I slapped the book shut. No way. No friggin' way! Mom, queen of MacDonald genealogy, was certain that Flora did not leave behind any progeny who passed their genetic material down to me. It is possible that one of my ancestors *met* Flora MacDonald during North Carolina's colonial days. But there was no way I had gotten some kind of psycho, ancestral-genetic vibes from Flora by looking at that photo.

I flipped back to the photograph of Dunstaffnage Castle. And once again I felt a frozen fingernail tracing down my spine.

Clenching my teeth, I forced myself to read the rest of the caption. "In the fifteenth century Dunstaffnage Castle became one of the strongholds of the Clan Campbell. Numerous raids against their enemies, the MacDonalds, were launched from this fortress. . . ."

The fine hairs on the back of my neck began to prickle. I swallowed hard and kept reading.

"The castle guards the narrow passage between Loch Etive and the Atlantic Ocean. Jane Campbell, called the Black Bitch of Dunstaffnage, once marooned a group of MacDonalds on rocks in the loch at low tide and let them drown. Other accounts claim she sent MacDonalds out to sea in leaky boats with no sails or oars."

My blood had turned to snowmelt. Nausea curled in my stomach. A faint roaring noise seemed to echo in my brain. This wasn't your standard tale of atrocities committed by the Campbell warriors. This was woman stuff, Campbell against MacDonald.

Chapter 13

I dropped the book on the table and bolted from the bookseller's tent. Gulping sunshine, jostled by the crowd, I tried to calm down. "This is absurd," I muttered, prompting a wary look from a man in Viking attire with a big MacKay emblem tattooed on his shoulder. "*I* am not the weird one here," I snapped, but he clearly wasn't convinced.

Me neither. I paced the grounds until it was time to catch up with Miguel again. We found seats at the main field, but the men's caber toss was underway and the atmosphere was so chaotic I didn't try to talk with him about anything serious. Like the possibility that my dislike of Christina Campbell might, just might, have something to do with the fact that centuries ago her ancestors and mine had hated each other's guts.

I waved at Randy, Charles, and Glen, and tried to focus on the field. Each man in turn hefted the caber upright, staggered a few steps to build momentum, then attempted to hurl it end over end, grunting or roaring with the effort. "Ahhh!" the crowd gasped whenever someone managed a proper toss. "Ohhh," it chorused when a caber fell askew. We even got one good "Ooohhh!" as an athlete lost control and staggered backwards with his caber in the direction of a pipe band. The pipers scattered, but no one came to any harm.

I was too distracted to even notice how fine Randy looked in his kilt. Miguel whooped and hollered whenever a particularly good toss was completed and jumped to his feet in alarm when the pipe band was threatened. As for me, I clapped on cue. But through it all this creepy thing buzzed in the back of my mind.

"Miguel," I said finally, when I couldn't hold it in anymore.

"Oh, great throw!" he cried, applauding wildly.

"Miguel!"

He looked at me, startled. "What?"

I couldn't go through with it. "Nothing."

He made an annoyed face at me, then swung his gaze back to the field. "Look at that guy—*geez!* I thought he had it."

"Miguel."

"What?" he demanded, glaring.

"Tell me more about this ancestral memory thing."

He slowly raised one thin black eyebrow.

I've always envied people who can do that. "Please! Just tell me."

"Well, I'm no expert or anything, but it makes sense

to me. The idea is that you can access memories—such as being comforted by a campfire—from your ancestors."

"You mean like channeling, or something? That's just bizarre."

He regarded me coolly for a moment. The crowd around us erupted for another good caber toss. "Do you want to know or not?" Miguel asked finally.

I sighed. "I truly want to know."

"It's not New Age drivel. We're talking science." He sounded aggrieved.

I studied my toes. "I'm sorry. Go on."

"O.K., here's another example. For years, marine biologists have wondered why whales sometimes beach themselves. Well, evidence suggests that millions of years ago, the ancestors of today's whales inhabited land. Whales slowly evolved into purely sea creatures, but that memory remains. Every once in a while something in a specific whale kicks in and sends him back to land."

"But that just sounds like—like instinct. That's not the same as real memories."

"I was giving you a very simple example to begin with." Miguel's tone was lofty. "Besides, what *is* instinct? How does a baby deer, too young to have any memories, know to run from a wolf?"

I wiped a trickle of sweat from the back of my neck. This climate was going to do me in. "But can you apply the same general principal to humans?"

"I think so. I got interested in this when I read an article written by a man whose daughter, maybe four years old, described a funeral in detail, even though she'd never been to a funeral. The man realized his daughter was re-membering a particular funeral that *he* had attended, forty years earlier."

"But—"

"That's an unusual example," Miguel said, waving away my protest. "Most of us don't access specifics. In broader terms, though, genetic memory can explain why some people feel compelled to get involved in Civil War reenacting, for example, and others are attracted to Highland Games. Or why some people love mountains and others the ocean. Why some authors write historical fiction, and others write murder mysteries. *Something* compels them to keep revisiting a particular time or geo-graphic area or theme. I think truly profound events or experiences or emotions are most likely to reverberate down through time."

I rubbed my arms. This still sounded too mumbo jumbo for me. "So you're saying that everything that ever happened to every one of my ancestors is somewhere inside me."

"No. Having everything *would* involve channeling, or past-life regression, or something. Your mother passed along what she had experienced up to the day you were born. Or maybe the day you were conceived," he amended, scratching the corner of his mouth pensively. "H'm. I wonder—"

"So how come I can't remember anything?"

"Because we don't know how to access the memories."

"If we don't know how to access them, then how can you say that these memories are why people get attracted to this whole Scottish thing?" I truly wasn't trying to be irritating. I was trying to understand something as alien to me as—as space abduction.

"You are something, you know that?" He shook his head. "Look, I don't have all the answers. Different people have different theories. But some scientists believe that one day we *will* know how to turn the key and unlock all that material. Won't that be great?" He grinned thoughtfully, forgetting me for a few seconds. Then he regarded me again. "In the meantime, very strong emotions still may reach through. The first time I heard bagpipes playing, I just *knew* I'd heard them before."

I massaged the growing tension in the back of my neck.

"Why the sudden interest?" Miguel picked at a nubbin of wool sticking out of his kilt.

I opened my mouth, then shut it again. Part of me wanted to tell him about the way I'd felt, looking at the photograph of Dunstaffnage Castle. About finding out that centuries ago, Campbells and MacDonalds *had* fought in some kind of fierce blood feud. And that the women were not just passive bystanders, waiting helplessly at home. And that as stupid as it sounded, this information was the only thing I'd stumbled over that might explain my instantaneous, bone-deep dislike of Christina Campbell. After all, Miguel was the only person I could think of who wouldn't laugh out loud at the very idea.

But I couldn't do it. "Just curious," I mumbled. "Come on. I want to show you the women athletes."

I bought us each a lemonade and took Miguel round to Field B. We watched Sheila and a half-dozen other women hurling stones and tossing sheaves and generally kicking butt. "Unbelievable," Miguel said admiringly, when the women's caber toss began.

I thought so, too. For a while I forgot about bagpipes and Christina Campbell and genetic memory and did what I was born to do, capture great images on videotape. I switched the automatic exposure to a high-speed shutter setting, and the crowd here was so thin I could play with angles, and I got some *great* stuff.

As I rejoined Miguel, he looked at his watch. "Two-thirty! I gotta run and get ready."

"Are you competing this afternoon?" I put the lens cap back on the camcorder.

He looked surprised. "No! I've got to meet the other guys and get formed up for the massed band concert."

I blanched. "The what?"

"Oh, come on. You've never seen the massed bands?"

"We were day visitors last year. We'd come for just a few hours. What's this about massed bands?"

"All the pipe bands come together on the field. Once today, and once tomorrow."

"And how many bagpipes is that all together?"

He considered. "Maybe . . . oh, I'd say about two hundred."

"Oh—my—God."

"Tanya, it's incredible! You've gotta come!"

"No way." I shook my head.

He grabbed my arm. "It's the heart of the Highland Games! You can't pretend to make a documentary without taping the massed bands!"

Pretend to make a documentary.

"I have spent the day listening to bagpipes," I snapped. "Pip*ers* and pipe *bands* and pipe *competitions* and pipe *concerts*. My head is already aching, and my bones are already quivering. I most certainly, definitely, unequivocally will not make a point of listening to two hundred damn bagpipes being played at once!"

Miguel stood in the dirt beside Field B and stared at me. Over his shoulder I saw a lithe Amazon hurl a caber and again wished like anything that I could hurl something, too. But maybe I'd already hurled enough, for the moment. Miguel seemed to think so. He hitched one shoulder toward the sky and let it drop.

Then he walked away.

A brittle feeling beneath my ribs threatened to crush my breathing, or rise up in my throat to choke me. I whirled and stomped off in the opposite direction.

I didn't think I could run far enough in half an hour to get away from two hundred manic bagpipers. So I did the only thing I could think of. I went to the campsite, found Mom's keys, and fired up the car. With windows rolled tight, air conditioner on, I cranked up the radio. I found some station playing the new glitzy country, which I am not fond of, and let it blare.

The campground seemed deserted. Everyone must be at the massed band concert, the heart of the Highland Games. Everyone but me. For a long time I stared blindly through the windshield at the lane running between the rows of sites. When I realized that my fists were clenched, I forced them open, pressing them flat against my thighs. Later, when I thought I heard a distant quiver of bagpipe noise, I turned the radio up another notch. Songs about broken hearts, commercials for septic tanks, it didn't much matter.

Finally I closed my eyes and leaned back against the headrest, and tried to let everything go. I felt lower than a tick turd. It doesn't matter, I told myself. It doesn't matter. *Forward.* It doesn't matter. . . .

I think I was asleep when someone banged against the

window. I jerked awake and cracked my knee against the steering wheel. "What the . . ."

A man stood beside the car, gesturing. "Tanya!" he mouthed through the window. Or maybe he was yelling. It was hard to tell.

I felt my hands curl back into fists. It was my father.

Chapter 14

I took a deep breath, turned off the radio, and opened the door. "Hey, Dad." I stared at his shoes. Brand-new Adidas. He used to live in loafers.

"What on earth were you doing?"

"Just listening to the radio." I cocked a cautious ear toward the festival grounds, but I wasn't borne away on a tidal wave of piping. The massed bands thing must be over.

My dad stepped closer and gave me an awkward hug. I stood like a tree, and his arms dropped. "How are you, Tanya?"

"O.K." I regarded him, this man who'd given me life. He'd put on a couple of pounds since I'd seen him last, and had gotten new glasses, and was wearing a red-checked shirt I didn't remember. For some reason I thought about genetic memory and almost freaked—some of his memories I definitely did *not* want—but then I remembered that our connection got installed the day I was conceived, or possibly born. Either way, I was safe.

"Where are your mother and Nancy?"

"*Nanag* is probably at the dance pavilion, and Mom's probably at the clan tent."

"I wasn't sure where to look. So I thought I'd start here. I figured I'd recognize the car. I just didn't know I'd find you in it."

I shrugged again. "This Highland heritage stuff isn't really my thing."

He took a tentative step forward. "Tanya, you know you're welcome to spend some time with me this summer. Nan's going to come for a couple of weeks. Judy would be glad to—"

"I'm O.K. here in North Carolina." Judy was The One. Dad's new wife. It would be impossible for me to care less about how Judy felt.

Dad slid his hands into his pockets. "We have plenty of room. We've got a guest room. You wouldn't have to share with Ryan or anything."

"Well, I am so glad to know that I don't have to share anything with Ryan," I said, icicle sharp and just as cold.

Dad's cheeks flushed red as raw beef.

Ryan is Judy's little boy. I'd never met him. I didn't even know for sure how old he was. But the one time I'd tried calling Dad, after the dust settled, Ryan answered the phone. I was already nervous about making the call, and when I heard this little kid on the other end of the line, I almost hung up. I didn't. I asked to speak to James Zeshonski.

The phone clunked down. In the distance, I heard Ryan shouting, "Papa Jim! Papa Jim! The phone's for you!"

Then I heard Dad say, "Thanks, little man!" Ryan erupted into sudden squeals of laughter. "No, no!" he shrieked. "Put me down! Don't tickle me!" The laughter faded away, but my dad was still chuckling when he picked up the phone. "Hello?"

Wordless, I clenched the receiver. "Hello?" he said again. I pressed my finger on the disconnect button.

I had never tried to call him again.

"Why don't I show you where the dance pavilion is," I said, breaking the awkward silence. Dad nodded.

I led the way through the campground, past the grandstand and the vendor tents. I skirted the Glen O' the Clans by a wide berth. If I could shield Mom from Dad during what I assumed would be a very brief visit, I would.

"So, are you still having fun playing with the video camera?" Dad asked, a note of forced and artificial cheer in his voice.

"I'm not *playing*," I said through clenched teeth. "I'm learning to make documentaries. I'd be farther along if I could have taken that second internship at the station in Green Bay. There aren't any television stations in Laurinburg."

"I didn't mean to be disparaging," he said quietly. "I

know it's a sincere interest, Tanya, and you have my support."

This was new. "Well . . . thanks."

"I would never suggest that you give it up. I just don't think you should spend *all* of your time hiding behind a camera."

I stopped dead, using every ounce of self-control to keep from exploding. I managed to point toward the dance area. "I'm sure Nan's down there."

He stood still, staring at me with his mouth twisted sideways. He always did that when he was thinking hard. "Tanya," he said finally, "I don't want things to be this way."

I hugged my arms close to my chest. "I don't, either. But I didn't start this."

Tiny wrinkles appeared between his eyebrows. "Tanya, you're not being fair—"

"Dad, I *know* what happened!" I hissed. Two passing dancers glanced our way, and I lowered my voice. "I know why you and Mom broke up. I know about Mom coming home and finding—what she found. So do *not* talk to me about being fair."

His cheeks turned that raw beef shade again, but he didn't look away. His chest rose and fell as he drew in a very deep breath, then blew it out again.

I jerked my head toward the rows of benches. "I haven't told Nan, by the way. She'll be glad to see you."

I left him there. A tight fist clutched my heart as I

marched away. I felt ready to explode. My eyes ached, but no tears came.

Finally I muttered a curse and jerked to a stop. I was standing near a whiskey vendor giving out free samples of Scotch, and everyone in the jostling crowd around me seemed *way* too happy. I was surrounded by happy people in plaid.

I forced myself to take a few deep breaths of my own. In and out. In and out. I don't know how long I stood there, a stalled trout in the Scottish stream. Finally I started wandering again.

And I wandered for the rest of the afternoon. The camera bag was a dead weight over my shoulder. I didn't have the energy to shoot a frame—which, since my documentary had pretty much come unraveled anyway, would not be an overwhelming loss to the public television community. I didn't even have the energy to eat shortbread. All I wanted to do was kill time until Dad left—either back to the airport or, if he was actually staying over, back to his hotel.

Finally I trudged through the parked cars and sat by Pond Scum Pond until the Games officially closed for the day and the parade of cars taking people from the field had crept merrily away. Then I plodded back through the grounds to the campsite.

Where I found Dad.

He and Nan were sitting at the card table. Nan was

chattering happily, her face open and trusting. Watching the two of them together made me feel like a plate of haggis. It was too late to undo the hurt Dad had caused Mom, but I was scared sick that he might break Nan's heart, too.

Mom was rummaging in the big cooler by the car. She looked a little flushed, but otherwise composed. I crouched down beside her. "Mom. What's *he* doing here?"

She glanced over her shoulder, then back at me. "You knew he was coming—"

"But I didn't know he'd stay past regular hours!"

"Keep your voice down," Mom muttered. "Nan invited your father to stay for supper. I said it was O.K."

"Mom—"

She tucked a loose strand of hair behind her ear. "We can do this. We can be civil. Your father and I want to make things as easy as we can for you girls."

"I can't do it, Mom. I can't sit down and share a meal with him."

She turned on me. "Tanya! I expect you to put some effort into this. For Nan's sake, if not your own. Understood?"

I wanted to do it. For Nan, and for my mother. But I just—could—not.

So I took the only recourse left. I lied. "But I had other plans this evening. I was coming to tell you. I got invited to have dinner with someone."

Her wise eyes narrowed. "Who?"

"This guy I met. We've been hanging out sometimes. He's from Clan Armstrong," I added, hoping that might lend credence to my story.

"You haven't mentioned him. What's his name?"

"Miguel Moreno. He plays the bagpipes. He's from Puerto Rico."

I'm a decent liar, but I couldn't possibly have made that up. Mom fingered her lower lip between thumb and forefinger, considering. "Where are you having dinner? I don't want you leaving the grounds."

"He and his grandmother are camping here. I won't leave the grounds."

Behind us, Nan's voice rose in excitement. "And the judge said I showed uncommon grace for a beginner. That's what she said, 'Uncommon grace.'"

"I want to meet this Miguel and his grandmother," Mom said.

"Sure!" I said brightly, fully aware of the likelihood of that promise biting me in the butt. "I'll bring them by sometime." And then I escaped.

I walked briskly down the lane without looking back. When I was sure I was out of sight, I leaned against a tree, considering. Seeing Dad had made me lose my appetite, but skipping out on dinner made me suddenly ravenous. The food vendors were closed. Miguel most certainly had *not* invited me to dinner. I didn't know if he was even speaking to me. I watched a woman at a nearby campsite tossing salad greens—what looked like frisee and endive and chard, not just measly old iceberg lettuce—and tried not to panic. Finally, with my metaphorical tail between my legs, I began wandering the campgrounds in search of Miguel.

As I ambled, trying to peer discreetly into each campsite, I heard lots of laughter. Impromptu Scottish jam sessions spilled singing and drumming and tunes from the small uilleann pipes into the evening. I smelled barbecued chicken and grilled hot dogs and fried potatoes. I saw families, and groups of friends, and whole clusters of sites devoted to one blasted clan or another. No one else was wandering, lonely and forlorn, in search of a meal.

I had almost given up when I spotted Miguel. His campsite was in the unfortunate end row marked by orange snow fencing, with no trees for shade or privacy. A big canvas tent stood in one corner of the site. Miguel sat at a table covered with a yellow paper cloth, playing cards with an elderly woman in a green sweat suit. I recognized his grandma from the clan parade. A beat-up Saturn was parked in their spot, and I paused beside it, hands shoved in pockets.

Miguel and his grandmother were playing double solitaire, and he didn't notice me right away. But finally he glanced up.

"Hey," I said.

"Hey." Miguel stood, looking uncertain, then beckoned me over. "Come meet my grandmother."

Grandma Dokken was a feather pillow of a woman, as soft and light as Miguel was skinny and dark. She had the habit of widening her eyes now and then when she talked, so when she asked, "Would you like some chocolate-covered graham crackers?" she seemed to be offering a rare delicacy.

Guilt nibbled my gut, but I was too hungry to say no. Fortunately, Miguel was too polite to tell his grandma that I'd pissed him off royally last time we spoke by cursing his instrument of choice and refusing to come to the massed bands extravaganza. "Yes, please," I said, and soon I was ensconced in a plastic lawn chair eating chocolate grahams.

I've had worse dinners and figured I'd last until morning after all, but a half-hour later Grandma D. said something about supper and invited me to stay. Woohoo! The chocolate grahams were just appetizers! Miguel fixed cheeseburgers, and I got a cheese sandwich and a baked potato out of the deal. I had no complaints. I made sure to pitch in with the dishes, which we washed in a hubcap because they'd forgotten to bring a dishpan, and I tried to be extra helpful by mentioning that making check-off lists in a spiral notebook can be useful for tracking things like camping gear.

"I'm sure you're right!" Grandma Dokken said with

that twinkling look of delight. "Now, my friend Betty offered me a canasta game with the Frasers. I do believe I'll wander over. It was good to meet you, Tanya."

After she left, Miguel and I stood in awkward silence for a moment. "Your grandma is nice," I tried.

"Yeah. It's good to see her enjoy herself. My grandfather died of Lou Gehrig's disease. She had some bad years."

I wasn't sure where that came from. Miguel sounded defensive, as if he wanted to let me know that while *he* might put up with my bad moods, he wouldn't let me lay any of it on his grandmother.

I dropped back into one of the lawn chairs. "I, um, guess I owe you an apology."

He sank down more slowly. He'd changed from his kilt into jeans and a Natural Resources Defense Council sweatshirt, which made him look more normal. "Tanya—"

"I know! I'm sorry. I was rude before, about that massed band thing. Although you were kinda rude about my documentary, too."

His forehead wrinkled. "I was? I didn't mean to be."

"Well, it wasn't the best conversation. And then I show up for supper. Which I do appreciate, by the way. More than you know."

"You're welcome, I think," Miguel said, eyeing me dubiously. "I could tell my grandma liked you. Although she hasn't seen your . . . your prickly side." He snorted with sudden, suppressed laughter.

"What?" I demanded. I tried to keep the irritation from my voice—I wanted to finish one apology before pissing him off all over again—but I did not see the joke.

"Prickly," he sniggered.

"What are you talking about?"

"Genetic memory. Maybe you're descended from a Scottish thistle."

I made a noise halfway between a sigh and a laugh. "I'll remind you that thistles supposedly kept invaders from Scotland's sacred soil and saved a bunch of Highland arses. Probably some Lowland arses, too."

"Probably," he said agreeably, and we both laughed again. I couldn't remember the last time I had laughed, and it felt strange, but I couldn't stop. I snickered and snorted, and right in the middle of it I said, "My dad's here. He's at my campsite."

Miguel's laughter died away, and he got this thoughtful look on his face. I was already regretting my words. I felt my stomach muscles cramp up, walling off any personal questions or recriminations. But he just nodded. For a moment the only sound came from the next campsite, where some mother yelled at some kid named Bruce to pick up his shoes.

"I think my grandmother's got a bag of marshmallows somewhere," Miguel said finally. "You wanna roast some?"

I flashed back to second grade, when Dad helped my Brownie Scout troop roast marshmallows in our backyard, and for a moment I felt a cold sadness. But for the first time, I was able to truly push bad memories aside. "Sure," I told Miguel. "I'd love to roast marshmallows."

So he found marshmallows and forks, and I built up the campfire. I must admit, something about the campfire *was* comforting, despite the sulky air. Miguel toasted his marshmallows to a light golden brown, and I thrust mine in the fire and brought them back flaming and scorched. We squashed them between the last of the chocolate graham crackers, and licked our fingers, and stared at the flames.

And we talked. Miguel told me about the influence of herbicides on aquatic ecosystems, and about thermal pollution. "I want to help people in developing countries have better access to fresh drinking water."

I told him about wanting to get into a good film school. "I'm going to be an independent filmmaker. I'm not just fooling around. This is for real."

"I do think that's cool." Miguel stabbed another marshmallow on his fork. "Truly."

"My dad doesn't." I stared at the flames. "He thinks I'm 'hiding behind a camera.' That's a quote."

"Oh."

"He used to be the absent-minded professor, and all of a sudden he got into theater like it's some new religion or something." I paused, thinking back to the strange experience of watching my dad sing and dance, wearing stage makeup so heavy it looked like he'd applied it with a trowel. "Now he wants me to take drama lessons. He says it will build my self-confidence."

"Are you going to do it?"

"No! Videography gives me all the self-confidence I need. It's a lot harder than people think."

"So is playing the bagpipes," Miguel said. "There are only nine notes, but we embellish them with throw notes and grace notes and strikes and stuff. The fingering is *very* challenging."

"I imagine so," I said. I owed him that.

By the time I said good night and wandered back to my own campsite, well past dark, Dad was gone.

Chapter 15

I forgot my brief flash of generosity toward Miguel's beloved pipes when I woke that Sunday morning to the sound of skirling.

The shrill scream of a bagpipes' chanter is so distinctive that it has its own noun: skirl. I read that somewhere, probably on a program at one of the Highland Games Mom and Nan had dragged me to the summer before. I haven't checked Webster's, but I'll wager a peanut butter pie that the words "shriek" and "blare" show up somewhere in the definition.

Anyway, my day began with some bloody piper walking through the campground playing his bloody bagpipes. "Somebody stifle him," I muttered, burrowing down in my sleeping bag.

"It's time to get up anyway, Tanya." Mom's voice came from above, and I realized that she was already up and about, just leaning back into the tent to roust me. "Nan and I want to go to the service."

"Service" no doubt meant something quaint like "kirkin' o' the tartan"—a vaguely Presbyterian service complete with bagpipes and Scottish blessings. "Go without me."

"Tanya." Mom's voice held a note of warning. When I didn't answer, she crawled back into the tent. I could hear Nan singing, "The sun will come out tomorrow," beyond the nylon.

I sat up and pushed my hair from my face. "I'm just too tired, Mom. I didn't get any sleep last night. Nan's snoring—"

"Yes, I know." Mom folded her arms, regarding me. She was already dressed in light wool trousers and a white blouse, with a MacDonald tartan sash secured with a MacDonald crest pin over her right shoulder. "Tanya, we need to have A Talk."

I'm not a coffee drinker, but I suddenly understood why some people crave the stuff. It is difficult to face A Talk when still feeling fuzzy as a Highland sheep. "Can it wait until we get home?" I mumbled. We'd be home that night.

"No. Tanya, your father has a hotel room in Fayetteville, and he will be back here today. I know Nan would be happy if he spent the whole day with her, but you need to talk to him."

I hunched over, elbows on knees, rubbing my eyes. "Why?"

"Because he's your father."

"I don't have anything to say to him."

"I think you do." She abruptly leaned forward and kissed my forehead.

Suddenly Nan appeared in front of the tent, looking chipper and well rested. "Don't forget, Tanya, the Highland fling exhibition is at ten-thirty."

I buried my face in my pillow.

"You promised!" she wailed. "You promised you'd dance with me."

"I *will*," I mumbled. "Meet me here at ten-fifteen."

That promise of incredible goodwill earned me a "get out of kirk free" card from Mom. "Since you're so tired, Tanya, Nan and I will go on to service without you. You can catch up with us if you want."

I didn't want. I took as much of a bath as a jug of water and washcloth will allow, and pulled on a pair of shorts and a clean shirt. The breakfast menu revolved around Pop-Tarts. As I choked one down, the piper came back through. I almost let fly with an apple frosted.

I was still feeling groggy, but in truth, Nan's snoring was only part of the problem. Sometime in the middle of the night, when I couldn't lie awake and listen any longer, I had crept out of the tent. I grabbed a flashlight and found that book I had purchased at The Proud Thistle. I ended up sitting in the car, reading, while the MacRowdies across the way got drunker and the rest of the campground tried to sleep.

I'd studied Bonnie Prince Charlie's failed uprising in

school, so I knew as much as the next kid about Highland warriors and the battle at Culloden. I knew that the British policy after the battle was brutal and that thousands of women were systematically turned out of their homes to watch their children starve. I knew the Scottish women had been victimized.

But the school textbook never mentioned Lady MacKintosh, who raised a regiment for the prince at age twenty-two and accompanied her husband to war with a pair of pistols. Or Isabel Haldane, who offered her apron to her hesitant husband and said, "Charles, if you are not willing to be commander of your men, stay home and I will go and command them myself." Or Margaret Murray, who cheerfully helped seize horses and money for the prince's cause from anyone reluctant to offer them freely. Or the nameless women who accompanied their men to war, giving birth in thickets or hauling toddlers along with an army that often traveled thirty miles a day, sometimes in deep snow and horrendous weather. Or the women who risked slaughter or arrest themselves by trying to help wounded men on the ghastly Culloden field, or by hiding their men after the battle.

My eyes had felt gritty by the time I laid my head back on the seat of the car. Scottish women in 1745 had formed their own opinions, made decisions for themselves and their children, supported their husbands in war or secretly worked against them if they felt it necessary. Lots of them were just girls, my age or even younger. There was something here I needed to think about.

By the time I'd crept from the car, even the Mac-Rowdies had gone quiet. I'd lost all track of time—

Geez! The time. I glanced at my watch, then quickly slammed my feet into my Birkenstocks. In a moment of marshmallow-induced weakness, I'd promised Miguel I'd come videotape his band during morning rehearsal.

When I arrived at the designated out-of-the-way lob-lolly pine, I found eight pipers and four drummers—all male, although there are women in some of the bands. They weren't kilted yet, this being a rehearsal, so I faced twelve guys of various sizes and shapes and ages sporting T-shirts that said things like "Pipers Do It with Amazing Grace" and "If It's Nae Scottish . . . It's Crrrr-ap!" Miguel spotted me and bounded over.

"Hey, cool!" he greeted me, obviously excited about his film debut. "Let me introduce you."

The leader of the Cross Creek Pines Pipe Band was a man named Dan Fielding. Dan had ripe apple cheeks and a bushy gray beard trimmed like British colonels' in old movies. "Young lady," he began without preamble, "we should start with a wee bit of history. It can rightly be said that the bagpipe is an instrument of remotest antiquity. In fact, it is the ancestor of the organ—"

A sandy-haired guy leaned into the shot. "The story *I* heard was that the Irish invented the bagpipes, but after hearing the music they sold it to the Scots." I pulled back and got a wide shot of them all yukking it up over that one.

Once they were sure I had acquired due awe of the complexities of their task, the band members fitted themselves with pipes and drums. As they jostled into a tight circle, facing inward, Mr. Fielding explained to me that the day's competition involved a five-minute medley. "Band—at the halt—quick march!" he barked.

The drummers raised their sticks and, at his signal, rattled a call to the pipers. They settled their pipes in place, and a low drone emerged into the morning. It quickly grew to a deafening blast force. And I stood ten feet away! I wondered how the band members could stand it. Maybe, I thought, they play in a circle so they can prop each other up, shoulder to shoulder. . . .

The thought started as a joke, but suddenly my hand began to shake and I had to stop tape. I stared at Miguel, standing tall in his place in the circle. For a moment I wanted like anything to stand there in that circle, be *part* of a circle, even if it meant learning to skirl.

"No, no." Mr. Fielding waved an arm and brought the noise to a discordant end. "Keep those doublings on the beat! Try it again from the low A."

I sucked in a lungful of pine-scented air. Get a *grip,* Zeshonski! I ordered myself. I didn't want to flip out right there in front of the Cross Creek Pines Pipe Band. If I didn't have a circle, I did have a video camera. I was an *independent* documentarian. Indies work alone.

So I got back to work. It was hard to find a good angle, but I managed to shoot over someone's shoulder and focus on Miguel. His face was set with concentration as he fingered the chanter and puffed air into the blowpipe and squeezed the bag. He was the only Latino in this tight circle of white guys. But they'd clearly accepted him as one of their own.

The ache near my sternum kicked in again. I waited until they reached the end of their piece, then caught Miguel's eye and gave a little wave to let him know I was leaving. He grinned and mouthed, "Picnic lunch?"

I nodded and made my mouth smile.

Chapter 16

*N*an waited eagerly while I wriggled into my kilt—an interesting maneuver when performed in a small tent. Our paternal unit had evidently not arrived from his hotel yet, which was fine by me, but I didn't upset Nan by mentioning him. This Highland fling thing meant a lot to her, and I wanted to get through it without undue stress for either one of us. Once my ghillies were laced and my hair crammed into a passable bun, we headed for the main field.

The Highland fling is very dear to loyal tartan hearts. "This is an exultant victory dance!" Miss Janet always reminded her students. "Dance for joy!" Small-scale exhibitions of other dances were scheduled for the end of the Games, during the dance awards ceremony, but that was too obscure for the national dance of Scotland. Organizers had invited all takers to assemble for one jolly massed fling. Nan and I arrived to find people already milling about the field —mostly women but a few men, too, both well-muscled competitors and barrel-shaped people who clearly danced, as Miss Janet so fervently wished, simply for the joy of it.

And suddenly I wanted to do that, too. No stage, no

judges, just me dancing a fling with my little sister. I could do this. I could dance and be happy.

I tried shouldering through the throng to the anonymity of center field, but Nan abruptly grabbed my wrist in a death grip and towed me forward. "Here is good," she whispered triumphantly.

A wave of ice water doused my feeble spark of hope. Nan had parked us behind Christina Campbell.

Christina stood casually with hands resting on her hips, chatting idly with another girl. Christina wore a black velvet jacket over her blouse today. Evidently Christina did not sweat. I stared at the back of her unwrinkled jacket, at her long white neck, and felt something ugly and harsh boil up inside.

"Isn't this turnout great?" a voice crackled over the loudspeaker. "Dancers, find some space. Spread out, make sure everyone's got plenty of room."

"Not here," I whispered fiercely to Nan, but she pretended she was deaf. I tried moving backwards and trod on someone's foot. "Sorry!" I said to a frizzy-permed mom flanked by twin girls with matching pigtails. When I edged to the right, I banged elbows with a tall red-haired girl wearing a competitor's number and a cool look of disdain. Nan was a wisp of immovable steel to my left.

I was hemmed in. Trapped. *Get over it, Zeshonski!* I tried ordering myself, sucking in air and fixing my gaze on a spot over Christina's right shoulder.

"Those of you in the stands are in for a real treat!" The announcer sounded deliriously happy. "This massed exhibition performance of the Highland fling will be a sight to behold! Dancers, get ready!"

The drone of bagpipes sliced the air. Christina shifted into the preparatory stance—head up, back straight, legs turned out. Nan followed suit, carefully mimicking Christina's every nuance. I forced my wooden limbs to remember what Miss Janet had taught me as the familiar tones of a strathspey bounced over the field. Bow. Rise to the balls of the feet, arms in first position. Disassemble onto left foot. Execute shedding movement with right foot. Spring to right foot.

In front of me Christina danced exultantly. Her raised arm formed a lovely arc, the fingers placed in perfect position. When she rotated a quarter turn, I glimpsed a serene smile. Christina was having a fine time. The twins behind me squealed with delight. They didn't have the concept of dancing in place down pat, but instead bounced about with unbridled exuberance, pressing close on my heels.

"Fling" means "kick" in Scottish parlance. When dancing a Highland fling, the dancer hops on each leg alternately while flinging the other in front and behind. I was already a beat late when I felt a small foot connect with my right calf.

"Ooh, sorry!" the little offender squeaked. Her sister giggled. I stumbled and got off-beat again. Christina had rotated back front, still graceful and precise—still perfect. Nan was a tiny mirror image. I could hear labored breathing and a muffled "oomph" somewhere behind me as novice dancers struggled to keep up.

And then it happened. The moment lasted forever, as if a maniacal director had ordered a videotape run in super slo-mo. Christina rotated another quarter turn, and I saw her in profile, dancing for the joy of it. I missed the turn. As we each kicked forward, my foot connected with hers. Hard.

She hopped wildly and ungracefully on her left foot. Once. Twice. Both arms flailed, but she couldn't catch her balance. She fell into her friend, who fell into the woman beyond her, a horrible chain of human dominoes.

And then Christina Campbell landed on her bonnie butt. Hard.

I had staggered backwards in my own struggle to stay upright and was vaguely aware of the flurry behind me as the twins and their mom tried to avoid disaster. But my gaze was locked on Christina's face as it turned to me. I saw bewilderment replaced by first recognition, then outrage, as she realized who had kicked her.

"Whoa, there!" the announcer blared, momentarily drowning out the music. "Looks like we had a little problem down in front. Keep your space, dancers."

The dancers closest to our little melodrama faltered, as if they didn't know whether they should keep flinging or stop and gawk. Nan had frozen, hands over her mouth in horror. Christina's jaw set in a hard line as she lurched to her feet.

Nan began to cry.

I beat feet and got the heck out of Dodge. It wasn't easy, elbowing my way through a hopping mass of Highland flingers. But I managed it somehow, without— I desperately hoped—knocking anyone else off their feet. I didn't look back.

Instead, my brain kept rewinding the videotape so that relentless images flashed in my mind: my final kick, Christina's fall, the look on Nan's face. I plunged into the festival crowd and lit out blindly. As I neared the refreshment booths, I was still so focused on the mental footage of Christina falling that I screamed like a hyena when a man's hand locked around my wrist.

"Tanya?" my father demanded angrily. "What on earth is the matter with you?"

I blinked at him. A number of onlookers, attracted by my stupid scream, looked curious. My dad just looked pissed.

"Tanya?" he asked again. "I am *talking* to you. I called your name twice, and you marched right past!"

A big man in a purple plaid kilt, with black leather vest and knee-high boots, frowned and stepped closer. He looked like a member of Clan Hell's Angels. "Is everything here all right?"

"It—it's O.K.," I stammered.

The man frowned at my father. A crowd was forming. "I saw him grab her," a girl with blue-streaked hair said helpfully. "And then she screamed," a little boy added, even more helpfully. A middle-aged lady wearing tight Capri pants pulled a cell phone from her purse and flipped it open.

"We're *fine*," I yelled. I wrenched my arm from my father's grip and lunged back through the crowd before that lady could dial 9-1-1. I knew Dad was following, but I didn't stop until I'd turned the corner and the whiskey seller's tent blocked us from the onlookers' view.

Dad stood there regarding me, his mouth twisted to one side, his jaw set. "You and I," he said finally, "are going to have A Talk. Over there." He pointed to an empty picnic table behind the line of food vendors' tents.

I followed him over and plunked down on the bench.

He sat on the other side, still looking pissed. "First of all," he growled, "I expect this cold shoulder treatment to stop. *Immediately.* I have tried to respect your wishes and give you space. I've tried to give you time to adjust to the divorce."

My brain felt like sludge. I watched him talk and was reminded of the way Charlie Brown's teacher talks in the TV specials. Blah blah blah.

". . . a long way to get here," he was saying. "Now kindly tell me what is the *matter.* And I want the truth."

What was I supposed to say? That genetic memory

was affecting my relationship with Nanag's idol? I folded my arms. "I've kinda got a lot on my mind," I mumbled.

His face turned that beef-liver color again, and I half expected to see steam coming out of his ears. But then white blotches stained his cheeks. That, I figured, was a really bad sign.

"Tanya MacDonald Zeshonski," he said in a voice so low I could barely hear him, "I am out of patience."

"Well, so am I!" Suddenly all of the brain sludge disappeared, and Christina Campbell seemed like small potatoes. "Didn't you hear me yesterday? I *know* what happened, Dad. I know why you and Mom got divorced."

He drew a long, deep breath. "You don't know everything you think you know. I've made some mistakes—"

"Mistakes?" He made it sound like he forgot to pick up milk on the way home. "How could you do that to Mom?"

"I'm not here to discuss your mother. This is not about her."

"Well, it is to me! She's really hurting, Dad."

His mouth twisted to the side. "She seems to be doing O.K."

"How can you say that? You don't know. You're not here to see. She's *suffering*. She's never going to get over this." I glared at him.

He held my gaze. Against my will, I blinked first. Swallowing hard, I stared down at the table. Someone had carved "Darla was here" into the wood in crude capital letters. I wondered if Darla had felt more real, like she mattered, after doing that.

He sighed. "I'm still your father, Tanya."

"Yeah? Well, maybe you should have thought about that before running out. You can't just turn your back on your wife and expect your kids to act like nothing happened." I rubbed my temples.

"I don't expect you to act like nothing happened," Dad snapped. "But I do expect you to put a little effort into maintaining a relationship with me. You could send me an e-mail from time to time. Talk to me on the phone for more than thirty seconds when I call."

"Talk about what? Your latest play?"

He stiffened. "Perhaps I share my news to fill the silence. I can't remember the last time you actually volunteered any news of your own."

And perhaps I can't bear to articulate my news: bad grades and not making friends and screwing up the sword dance. The effort of holding all that in made my head throb.

My silence let him keep rolling. "You were less than civil yesterday. And ten minutes ago you walked right in front of me, while I called your name, and acted for all the world like I didn't exist. I will not tolerate that behavior, Tanya. I'm still your father, and I deserve your—"

I slammed my palms on the table. "I don't *care* what you think you deserve! Do you care at all about what I deserve? Or does *everything* have to be about you?"

He looked as shocked as I felt by that little explosion. He stared at me, studied the crowd, looked at his hands. I wanted him to say, Of *course* I care about what you deserve! Why don't you start by telling me about the documentary you're working on? I want to hear all about it.

Encouraged by our sudden stillness, a scavenging chipmunk darted beneath the table in search of crumbs. The next table was noisily claimed by a happy family lugging a cooler. A piper wandered by, piping away. I suddenly understood why so many people wanted bagpipes played at funerals.

I stood up slowly, still hoping he'd stop me.

Then I walked away.

Chapter 17

I didn't stop moving until I reached our campsite, where I crawled into our tent and frantically tore off my kilt and vest. I threw the wool and velvet into the corner. The blouse I actually ripped apart with a harsh tearing sound that wasn't nearly harsh enough.

Finally I flopped back on my sleeping bag and crooked one elbow over my eyes. The good news: my exchange with Dad had blotted out the image of Christina Campbell's fall. The bad news: that memory now came rushing back.

What was *wrong* with me? I would forever be known as the girl who knocked Christina Campbell on her rear. Christina would never forgive me. Nan would never forgive me.

"It was an *accident!*" I muttered, but already a mental duel bounced between my ears:

You kicked Christina because you're jealous of her.

I did not! It was crowded, those little girls kicked me first—

You're angry because Nan admires her.

I am not! It's just this bizarre reaction I get whenever I see her. I can't explain it, unless—unless . . .

I groaned, bringing my fists to my forehead. I lay there for a long time, wrestling with two unacceptable choices. I simply could not embrace the notion that some musty genes had twitched, causing me to freak whenever I saw Christina Campbell. And yet, if that wasn't the case . . .

I might have stayed in the tent for the rest of the weekend if the stuffy confines hadn't been so blasted hot. When my sweat began to simmer, I gave up and pulled on my civvies. I planned to don dark glasses and spend the rest of the weekend burying myself in the thickest crowds I could find. But as I crawled from the tent, something hit my left shoulder. I looked down and saw a purple-and-white blob of pigeon poop on my shirt. The Scottish gods had provided a graphic metaphor of my performance in life.

The shirt was one of my favorites, white with a blue logo on the front from the Apostle Islands National Lakeshore. I wiped off what I could with a tissue, but it left a stain. With nothing clean available, I dug through the laundry bag and found my other shirts. I examined both wadded specimens. Let's just say that the bird-poop shirt was the best of the lot.

I considered. I was getting low on cash, and besides, I wasn't eager to buy a T-shirt that proclaimed something pithy like "Plaid to the Bone."

The only other thing I could think of prompted a muttered curse. I stalked to the Glen O' the Clans. When I reached the MacDonald tent, Mom gave me a wave from the front table where she was regaling a young family with some tale of MacDonald glory. I went behind the tent and scrabbled in the storage bins until I found one of the MacDonald sashes Mom kept trying to foist upon my unwilling shoulder. At least it covered up the bird poop.

"Oh no, dear." It was the Mrs. Santa Claus lady, who appeared around the corner of the tent as I tied the knot by my rib cage. "Sashes go over the *right* shoulder."

"This will be fine," I said, striving for sweet-but-firm, and fled. As I left, I caught Mom's gaze. Her look of surprised delight added to my increasingly bad mood. It wasn't even noon. The final day at the stupid Cross Creek Highland Games stretched out before me like a walk through the Mojave. Day's end seemed a long, long way away.

I wandered back to the performance area among the growing throngs of eager visitors. I was scanning the day's program, trying to find something worth videotaping, when I heard someone call my name.

"Tanya!" Miguel's grandma sauntered through the crowd, waving. She wore little white tennis shoes and a turquoise baseball cap and an ankle-length denim skirt. I do like old people who feel comfortable wearing denim. I'm hoping like anything that I don't descend into that gaping maw of polyester that seems to snare most women when they hit sixty or so.

"How are you this morning, dear?" Grandma Dokken asked.

"Did you happen to watch the Highland fling exhibition?" I asked warily.

"Why, no. I was watching the MacCranies and the MacDuffies in a tug-of-war match on the back field. Why?"

"Oh, no reason. I'm fine, ma'am. Just fine. And you?"

"Lovely!" she said, her eyes going wide in that manner she had, like she was confiding a wonderful secret. "Where are you headed?"

"Just wandering."

"Well, why don't you come along with me? One of my favorite folk singers is going to perform in a few minutes."

We made our way through the plaid masses and found seats in front of one of the folk stages. I got the camcorder out and loaded a new cassette. I didn't much feel like working, but at least it would give me something to do.

"Ah, that's right." Grandma D. regarded me with one of her delighted smiles. "You're making a documentary, yes?"

"Well . . . yes." I couldn't help feeling pleased by her choice of words—not "trying to make" or "pretending to make" or even "hoping to make." Still, I had to add, "But it's not going so well."

"Oh? Why is that?"

What could I say? I wasn't about to tell this nice lady, who was obviously having a fine time, that I had planned to make a documentary exposing Highland Games as a tartanized fantasy for clueless losers. "Let's just say my premise is evolving," I hedged.

"Oh?"

She sounded truly interested. I wasn't used to that. I shrugged, rubbing a smudge of dirt from one knuckle. "Well, I'm not really into all that Scottish heritage and stuff," I mumbled. "But last night I started reading this book about women in Scotland during the '45. I mean regular women, not Flora MacDonald. And it was pretty cool. Some of these women were really kick-ass!"

My face flamed as soon as the words left my mouth, but Grandma D. chuckled. "Don't mind. I'm all in favor of kick-ass women."

"Well, this book talked about women making up their own minds, not just doing whatever their husbands told them to. Some women took their children on the road with them so they could stay with their husbands when they went off to war. Some were spies, and some stood up to the British when the soldiers came to terrorize the civilians."

"That's a period I don't know very much about," Grandma D. confessed. "But it sounds fascinating."

"I'm not big on hero worship. Like the whole Flora Mac-Donald thing. But I like the idea of looking at everyday women, nameless women, and honoring what they did during such horrible times. I'm thinking about shifting focus and making a documentary about those women."

"Some of my friends remember when women weren't even allowed to march in the procession at Highland Games," Grandma D. confided. "That was just ten or twelve years ago. Everyone could use some reminding about Scottish *women's* place in history. I think your video sounds like a wonderful idea."

I chewed my lip for a moment. "Finding visuals will be tough, though. Maybe I can track down some old prints or paintings. . . ."

"Or use reenactments?"

"Possibly, if I can find reenactors who do a good job. You know, people who are very authentic in their clothing and stuff. And maybe I can get some footage from Scotland somehow. Scenic shots."

"That could work!" She nodded vigorously. "With landscape shots and a good script, you could encourage the audience to use their imaginations to fill in the gaps. That might be even more engaging."

I pulled out my notebook and scribbled some notes. I wasn't at all convinced that I could pull this off—I knew from hearing producers at WPNE whine that covering voice-over scripts about historical subjects could be a chore. Still, it was almost fun to sit on a hard wooden bench, baking in the sun, spitballing ideas for a documentary with Grandma Dokken.

We got interrupted when the folk singer took the stage. Her name was Fiona MacGregor—so darn Scottish I couldn't help wondering if she'd made it up. Still, as she tuned her guitar, I felt a tentative flicker of interest. A female performer would be more likely to know songs about historical women.

The benches were packed, and Fiona kept the faithful enthralled with a mixture of mournful ballads and what sounded like rollicking beer hall tunes, although beer isn't a Scot's drink of choice. And she did indeed include a couple of songs that had potential. My Panasonic has an external microphone jack, but there was too much ambient noise to try recording her then, so I jotted down the song titles. Maybe after the performance I could catch Fiona and ask her to sing them again in a quiet place.

After that my mind wandered, and I stopped listening, doodling notes instead. I'd have to see if The Proud Thistle's proprietor had any other relevant prints I could videotape.

Suddenly Fiona MacGregor jerked my attention back like a hooked musky. "Oh, cruel was the foe that raped Glencoe, and murdered the house of MacDonald," she sang.

A shiver rippled down my spine. No lie. It felt just like

the moment I'd looked at that photo of Dunstaffnage Castle. I darted a glance at Grandma D. She was listening attentively, but showed no signs of distress or chill.

Fiona's voice reached right inside me. "They came from Fort William with murder in mind; the Campbell had orders King William had signed. . . ."

The Campbell. This ballad was about more Campbells murdering more MacDonalds. I clenched the edge of my seat with my hands.

"They came in the night when the men were asleep. . . ."

It was ridiculous. It was *impossible.*

"Like murdering foxes among helpless sheep, they slaughtered the house of MacDonald. . . ."

Something pressed softly against the back of my throat. A fine sheen of sweat slicked my cold skin. I shuddered violently.

Grandma Dokken shot me a look, then frowned. "Are you all right, dear?" she whispered. "You've gone ghostly pale."

"I'm fine," I managed through clenched teeth.

Fiona sang, "Some died in their beds at the hand of the foe; some fled in the night and were lost in the snow. Some lived to accuse him who struck the first blow, but gone was the house of MacDonald. . . ."

The finger-against-the-throat sensation got worse, and suddenly the possibility of losing my breakfast seemed very real. I had to get out of there before I started spewing half-digested Pop-Tarts.

"Excuse me," I choked to Grandma D., and began stumbling past a wall of knees to get to the aisle. "Excuse me . . . pardon me . . . *please* excuse me!"

I only tromped on one or two feet before reaching the aisle. I bolted to the back just as Fiona MacGregor finished and the crowd erupted in applause. I hardly noticed. The ballad's refrain was echoing in my head.

I kept walking, trying not to be sick. Trying to shake off the willies and get my bearings. *I have to figure this out,* I thought. I wasn't sure what that meant, much less how to go about it. But I wanted some answers.

When someone tapped me on the shoulder, I about jumped out of my skin. I turned to face a short-haired woman wearing sensible shoes and a tartan sash over her white blouse. "Right is right," she said.

"I beg your pardon?" For a bizarre moment I thought this stranger had stopped me to say she agreed with my decision to pursue this Campbell-MacDonald thing.

But she plucked my sash. "You need to switch this to your right shoulder, dear. Remember, right is right."

I stared at her. Then I started to laugh. She looked startled and took a step backwards. I pushed one fist against my mouth and made myself stop laughing.

The woman disappeared into the crowd. I made my

way to clan row and approached the Clan MacDonald tent. I felt a flush of relief, which prompted another semi-hysterical outburst I controlled with some effort. For a long while I stood under a pine tree, leaning against the rough orange plates of bark. Somehow I'd become another MacDonald pilgrim, come to delve into clan history.

I watched Mom as she darted back and forth—greeting people, passing out membership brochures, pointing to MacDonald territory on a big map, offering her business cards. Good old Mom. Very sane. Very ordinary. After a while the last flush of nausea disappeared, and my heart stopped racing. I waited until Mom was between visitors, then went to say hi and surprise her with a quick peck on the cheek.

"Well, my goodness!" she said. "How are you, dear?"

"I'm O.K.," I lied. "How are you, Mom?"

"Well . . . fine," she said carefully. I could tell she was trying to figure out what was up with me. Nan must have talked with her about the Highland fling debacle by now.

"Mary?" It was that Doug guy, standing with a middle-aged couple. "I'm sorry to interrupt, but these people have some questions about genealogy. . . ."

Mom gave me a look. "Are you really O.K.?" she whispered.

I nodded. "Go on, Mom. I, um . . . I just came by to find a book on clan history."

Now Mom looked downright suspicious. "Well, you know what we have." She pointed to the row of books on the table.

I couldn't fix my parents' split or ask Mom to move back to Wisconsin. I couldn't change the adoration in Nan's eyes when she saw Christina or erase the searing memory of kicking Christina to the dust in front of hundreds of people. At this point I wasn't even sure I could pull a credible documentary out of my hat. But if I had to pore through every blinkin' book in Mom's clan library, I was going to discover what was behind the MacDonald-Campbell feud—and what that feud might possibly have to do with me.

While Mom got busy with the heritage seekers, I selected *A Considered History of Clan MacDonald* and retreated off to one side, out of the way. Sitting on a soft bed of dead pine needles, leaning against a tree trunk, I began to read.

Chapter 18

I didn't have to read every book in the clan library. The Great Feud formed an entire chapter in the *Considered History,* and it was a long chapter. The sounds of the Highland Games crowd faded as I turned the pages, my imagination racing back through the centuries. By the 1200s the mighty MacDonald and Campbell families were already sparring for power. In 1296 Sir Colin Campbell was ambushed and killed by a friend of the MacDonalds. Things went downhill from there.

When I finished the chapter, I slid the book back into place on the clan table at a moment when Mom was busy with visitors, and hurried away. I needed time to think about what I'd read. I cut through the grounds and arrived at Pond Scum Pond twenty minutes before noon.

After taking a few deep breaths, I lay on my back in the weeds, eyes closed, trying to block out the distant strains of bagpipes. Trying to relax. Trying to forget about feuds between Campbells and MacDonalds and between me and my dad.

It didn't seem to be working. Maybe I needed one of

those New Agey things, guided imagery or meditation or something. How did that work? I tried to pluck something helpful from my memory. "Om," I began, feeling like an absolute dork. "Om . . ."

"Hey."

I opened my eyes and saw Miguel standing against the summer sky, holding a bedraggled paper sack. He'd switched from jeans to his band kilt, and I jerked upright. I did *not* want to discover the age-old secret of what guys wore underneath. "Hey."

"What are you doing?" He plopped down on the grass beside me.

"Trying to meditate."

"Why?"

I hesitated, staring at the *Lemna minor* covering the pond. "I think," I said slowly, "I'm in danger of either having a stroke or losing it altogether."

"Really?" His forehead wrinkled. "Grandma said you got sick or something this morning. Are you O.K.?"

"No. I am not even remotely O.K."

"What's going on?"

I wrapped my arms around my knees, stared at the pond, and finally decided to begin with the (relatively) here and now. I told him about my dad's obsession with dinner theater and my mother's broken heart. Then I told him about the exchanges I'd had with my father since he'd arrived at the Games. "All he cares about is his latest play. He thinks that me knowing he cheated on Mom doesn't make any difference. He acts like I'm five years old and he can tell me what to do."

"That all pretty much sucks," Miguel said slowly. "My parents fight sometimes, but I can't imagine having everything explode like that. Wow."

"Yeah. Wow."

"Here." He began rummaging through his paper bag. "I brought lunch." He pulled out a meat pie wrapped in foil for himself, then handed me a fork and a plastic container. "My grandmother sent this for you."

I pulled off the lid. Salad. An honest-to-God salad, with tomatoes and carrots and cucumber slices, and even sunflower seeds and grated cheese. "Your grandmother," I said, "is a truly wonderful woman."

We ate in silence for a few minutes. The salad tasted heavenly. "I'll find your grandmother later and tell her I'm O.K.," I said finally. "And thank her for this in person. My mom and I didn't pack any salad stuff. We haven't camped out before."

"I guess your mom had a few other things on her mind." Miguel licked his fingers.

"Yeah." I shook my head. "I can't get mad at her. She's been through too much."

"You've been through a lot, too."

I shrugged. "Not like her."

A red-winged blackbird perched on a weed nearby,

squawked at the pond, then flew off. "When are you going to have it out with your dad?" Miguel asked.

I turned on him. "What do you mean? I've had it out with him already."

"Well . . . not really. Not from what you said. You told him you wanted to talk about *you,* but you didn't wait for him to answer."

"What do you know about it?" I shot him an irritated look. "I gave him plenty of time, and he just sat there staring at his fingernails."

"Maybe he's not so good at having hard conversations. Maybe you need to try again, force the issue."

"No," I said flatly. "I can't handle any more with him. Every time I'm *near* him, I get so worked up I can hardly breathe. Honest to God. It makes me feel like I'm going to explode."

Miguel folded a piece of aluminum foil carefully so the sloppy part was inside, then tucked it back into the bag. "O.K. Whatever you say."

We sat for a while longer. I tried to swallow this latest surge of anger. I didn't want to be pissed at Miguel, too. Somewhere behind us, from the parking area, I heard a father bellowing at some kid to *wait.*

"There's something else," I said finally.

"What's that?"

I took a deep breath and told him about Dunstaffnage Castle and Jane Campbell. "Just reading about this castle—which looks like something out of a bad dream, I might add—gave me the willies. And then I read about *her.*"

"This is awesome!" Miguel looked delighted.

"I'm glad you think so. There's more." I described the scene that morning during the concert. "The song was about some dark murderous deed done by Campbells against the MacDonalds. I got chills and then sick to my stomach."

"Like you were about to have a stroke again?"

"*No!* Aren't you listening? A stroke is tight chest and can't breathe. This was cold and nausea. They're very distinct."

The subtleties of my distress didn't seem to register on Miguel's concern meter. "What exactly did the Campbells do?"

"It was hard to tell exactly from the song lyrics, so I went back to the clan tent and read about it. Actually, this feud thing goes back centuries. And the MacDonalds did their share of slaying and pillaging." I rubbed my arms briskly. "But the ballad was about the most famous atrocity, called the Massacre of Glencoe. Back in 1692 a group of soldiers led by a Campbell came visiting a big MacDonald family. They received warm hospitality, dinner and cards and cozy beds, the whole nine yards. They stayed for over a week. But then the Campbell leader got a message from the king or somebody to bring 'fire and sword' to the place—"

"To burn and kill? Why?"

"I don't know. I skimmed over the politics. But the point is, at five one morning, the guests suddenly rose up and killed their hosts. About forty MacDonalds were butchered. Everyone else fled into the winter snows as the house burned down. A lot of them died of cold and starvation trying to make their way to safety. Evidently some MacDonalds still hold a grudge."

Miguel exhaled slowly. "No wonder you reacted so strongly to that Campbell girl—the dancer, what was her name?"

"Christina. And there's more." Staring at the pond, I told him about the Highland fling exhibition. "I *swear* it was an accident. People kept pressing in on us, and this little girl behind me kicked me twice, but—"

"But what?"

I leaned back on my hands. "O.K., here's the thing. You and I can talk about old feuds, but there is another possible explanation. I was only out there hopping around in the first place because Nan wanted me to. And once she spotted Christina, I might as well have been dog food." I shook my head. "Forget it. I don't want to talk about Christina."

He considered. "O.K., let's say that's still muddy ground. But the other stuff—the castle and the song—you gotta admit, that's pretty cool."

"It's freaky!" I protested weakly. "The idea that this ancient Scottish stuff could somehow . . . but I swear,

Miguel, I thought I was going to cough my cookies this morning when I heard that song. And I got cold, this morning and yesterday, too. It was *not* normal."

"You must be tapping back to the past. There's no other explanation."

"Then tell me this. There are *tons* of MacDonalds floating around this state. How come they all don't recoil in horror every time they see a Campbell?"

"Maybe you're descended from someone who actually experienced some Campbell atrocity against the MacDonalds and survived. Other MacDonalds, from other branches of the clan, wouldn't feel so strongly."

"But if I was, then Mom would be, too. And Nan. And Nan adores Christina."

"H'm. I see your point." Miguel beat a rhythm against one knee with his thumb. "Well, maybe the difference just comes down to random genetics. You know, like you inherited the particular genes for brown hair and long fingers and hating Campbells."

"I don't know. . . ."

"O.K., let's analyze this. Tell me again how you feel— physically—when something gets under your skin."

"Like bagpipe music?"

He rolled his eyes. "Like talking to your dad."

I considered. "Well, my chest gets tight, like I said. Sometimes I can hardly catch my breath. And my muscles clench up."

"And you said that when you heard about the Campbell-MacDonald feud—even when you just saw a picture of that castle, before you knew anything—you got chills and felt sick to your stomach."

"Right." I nodded slowly. I wasn't sure where this was going.

"O.K. Now think back, and try to remember how you felt the very first time you met Christina."

I clicked on a mental picture of Christina Campbell in that corridor at Highland High, when I backed into her. I saw her glowing smile, and her perfect turnout, and the way her father looked at her. "I just remember not liking her," I said finally, an edge of irritation in my voice. "I didn't know why. I felt my blood pressure go up. And my chest got tight." Suddenly I sat up straight. "But . . . I think I had *both* kinds of feelings. The air in that hallway felt cold. It had been like a steam bath in the ladies' room, and I remember thinking that they'd turned the A.C. on or something."

Miguel grinned. "What if that cold sensation didn't come from air conditioning? I really think there is something genetic between you two."

I made a face.

"Look at the bright side. It means you're not being just nasty when you see Christina and feel that way."

"Well, yeah. Maybe I truly can't help it."

"You can't! It's built into your genetic code!"

"In fact, I'm the victim here!" I was feeling better.

He snorted. "I wouldn't go that far. But it is intriguing."

I wasn't ready to describe the whole experience as "intriguing." But I'll be honest. Any explanation of my malicious streak, even this one, was better than nothing.

Miguel pushed to his feet. "I gotta get back to the band. We have to be in the final tune area ten minutes before competition so the officials don't have to look for us. Hey, will you do me a favor?"

"Sure."

"Videotape the massed bands performance this afternoon."

I stared at him. "A thousand pipers skirling at once? You have got to be kidding me!"

"No, I'm not," he said stubbornly. "I'd really like you to. I'm always in the middle of it. I never get to see what it looks like from the stands."

The words "No way!" quivered on the tip of my tongue, straining to be said. *Aching* to be said. But I couldn't help thinking that this weekend, horrible as it had been, would have been much worse without Miguel and his grandma.

"Well . . . I suppose I could do that," I said finally. "If I wear earplugs and take a few aspirin beforehand."

He grinned in triumph. "Great!"

We walked back through the rows of parked cars toward the grounds. The after-church crowd was still pouring in, a steady crawl of SUVs and cars inching across the field. The volunteers' smiles were beginning to look glazed as they waved people into place and gave directions to the porta-johns. I wasn't the only person ready to see the Cross Creek Highland Games wind to a speedy conclusion.

"You can probably find my grandmother at the campsite," Miguel told me before we parted company.

"Great. I'll return this." I waved the plastic container.

"And hey, Tanya. You really should talk to your father."

Chapter 19

I stomped toward the campground, pissed all over again. Miguel could be an extremely irritating person.

I found Grandma Dokken at her campsite, reading a romance novel and eating M&M's. "Tanya!" she exclaimed. "How nice to see you, dear. Did you enjoy your lunch?"

"Yes." I plopped into a lawn chair beside her. "I can't thank you enough for the salad. My mom didn't think it was a good idea to bring much fresh food, even with the cooler."

"Well, I tend to overdo," Grandma D. said, looking not the least bit apologetic. "Have some M&M's?" She poured a stream into my cupped hands. "Let's make sure you get lots of green ones. When Miguel was little, I used to tell him that the green ones tasted better than the rest." She gave me that eye-twinkling smile.

"Did he believe it?"

"Oh yes! In fact," she leaned closer conspiratorially, "I think he still does."

That perked me up a tad. "I'm sorry I disappeared on you this morning," I said. "All of a sudden I didn't feel well."

"Is everything all right?"

I picked at a string of frayed lemon-yellow webbing on my lawn chair. Maybe Grandma D. accepted the idea of genetic memory, just as Miguel did, but I wasn't ready to have *that* conversation all over again. "I've been uptight because my dad is here this weekend," I finally confessed. "He came down from Wisconsin. My mom and dad got divorced a few months ago."

"Oh, dear. I'm sorry to hear that."

"I'm worried about my mom. Having my father here stirs everything up for her again."

Grandma D. sighed, looking over the orange snow fence that marked the campsite. "I've never been divorced. But I remember how I felt when my first husband died—"

"Your *first* husband?" I felt my cheeks get hot. "I'm sorry. I just hadn't known you'd been married twice."

"My first marriage lasted only eight months. I was a nurse during the Korean War, and I married a G.I. A wonderful man named Joe. He was killed by a sniper."

"I'm so sorry!"

"It was a long time ago, dear."

We sat for a few minutes. A little kid tore up and down the lane on his bike shouting, "To infinity and beyond!" I tried to picture this elderly lady as a young nurse, wife, and widow in the filth and fear of the Korean War.

She patted my hand. "It was a terrible time. But I came home and eventually met someone else. Richard and I got married and had a beautiful daughter—Ellen,

Miguel's mother. I don't know what my life would have been like if Joe had lived—and he *deserved* to live—but I can't regret having Richard and Ellen and Miguel. Not for an instant."

I felt a wee bit ashamed of the pity pool I'd been back-stroking in all weekend. I ate another M&M. A green one. I think it *did* taste better than the others.

"I learned a lot about myself in Korea," Grandma Dokken said. "I learned how strong I could be when things got rough. I hope your mother finds that same reserve, dear."

I smiled at her. "Thank you. I hope so, too."

Grandma Dokken and I wandered back to the grounds together. When she asked about my plans, I said I wanted to look for historical prints at The Proud Thistle and check out the reenactors.

"Oh, for your documentary!" Grandma D. nodded. "Mind if I tag along?"

I was glad for the company, so we set off together. We did not, however, find an abundance of riches at The Proud Thistle. The proprietor showed us the obligatory prints of Flora MacDonald and Bonnie Prince Charlie. "And I can think of a few portraits of more prominent women," the man said, tipping his head thoughtfully. "In galleries. But that's about it."

"One print does not a documentary make," I muttered to Grandma Dokken as we went back outside.

"Never mind. Let's go talk to the reenactors."

We arrived at the reenactment area just in time to see a man wearing all nine yards of a great kilt, with some kind of blue paint smeared on his face, demonstrate the use of the round shield. "This targe includes a detachable spike," he explained, affixing a six-inch iron point to the shield's center. "With the spike in place, the targe is both weapon *and* defense."

"Wicked awesome!" a mesmerized boy breathed. I predicted that sales of reproduction targes were about to skyrocket at vendor row.

"Is this helpful?" Grandma D. whispered. She sounded dubious.

"Not really." I sighed, ready to acknowledge that my documentary was nothing more than a pile of crrrr-ap. "Let's go."

Grandma Dokken and I ended up at a demonstration of Scottish country dancing, which is very different from the competitive dancing Christina Campbell and Nan thrive on. Country dancing is more like social dancing. The emcee explained that it originated in the Lowlands. And a fiddler accompanied the dancers. No bagpipes in sight.

Eight couples demonstrated reels and jigs and strathspeys. The women wore white dresses with tartan sashes, and the men wore full Highland formal dress. Just *once,* I thought, I'd like to see a Scot wearing full *Lowland* formal dress. But I must have been getting tired, because the whole notion seemed less annoying now. Less important. Besides, I don't think there is such a thing as Lowland formal dress.

After the last round of applause died down, the announcer stepped up to the front again. "Our dancers are going to teach you all a few steps," he called. "On your feet, everyone!"

"Oh, what fun!" Grandma D. jumped up. "Come on, Tanya. Let's give it a try."

I hadn't evolved quite that far. "Um . . . I don't think so. I'll stay behind the camera."

The announcer succeeded in getting most of the audience down to the dance area. I positioned myself off to one side and focused in on Grandma Dokken. I couldn't help smiling as I watched this lovely woman in white tennies and turquoise baseball cap learning the steps, her skirt swirling around her ankles, smiling with delight as one of the kilted men offered his arm.

And a new idea suddenly crept into my head. My documentary was *not* in the toilet. I finally knew what my angle should be.

"I captured it all," I told Grandma D. when she joined me again.

"Oh, gracious." She laughed, still a little breathless.

"May I interview you sometime? For my documentary?"

"Me?" She looked surprised. "If you think it would be helpful, dear. I'm hardly an expert on Scottish culture, though. I can't think that I'll have anything worthwhile to say."

"I think you might."

"Well, if you say so." She looked at her watch. "We'll have to do it another time, though. We better head to the main field if we're going to get a good seat for the massed bands."

I gritted my teeth and tried to smile. "Lead on, MacDuff," I said, and she laughed again.

A flood of people was already washing toward the grandstands. The last round of athletic competitions was winding up, and a manic Border collie was racing around with a happy doggy grin on his face, and a blinding array of tartan flags and banners draped every possible vertical surface. I'd like to report that they snapped smartly in the breeze, but the truth is, they hung like wet dishrags. Still, it was a scene of veritable Scottish ecstasy.

I was scanning the bleachers when a youngish woman dressed in some vaguely ancient Celtic robe put a hand on my arm. "Your sash is on wrong," she whispered kindly. "Just switch it to the other shoulder."

"It's *fine.*" I turned away and took Grandma D.'s arm. "The top row of the bleachers would give me the best vantage for videotaping," I told her. I didn't mention that

I wanted to be as far away from the ranks of skirlers as possible. "Do you mind climbing?"

"Heavens, no. I'll just hang on to you."

We found space on the top row, midfield, right above a section reserved for "special guests." I scrabbled in the camera bag for a new battery and popped it in. "Mrs. Dokken, do you know what's up with the sash thing? Complete strangers keep stopping me to say I should be wearing it on my right shoulder instead of my left."

"Well, I have heard of the custom." Her eyes widened with amusement. "Technically, only the wife or daughter of a clan chief can wear a sash over the left shoulder. All other clan women wear it over the right."

"Oh." I digested that. What a joke—me, of all people, parading around impersonating Scottish royalty!

"I don't think it really matters," Grandma D. confided. "Some people get, well, a bit too wrapped up in *rules* for my tastes."

"For mine, too."

As if on cue, I heard someone a few rows below us say something about a chief. A gang of people wearing matching tartans filed in to the reserved seats. A gray-haired gentleman in full regalia waved in all directions before settling down on the bench. A little patter of applause rippled through our section.

"Who's that?" I whispered.

She consulted her program. "I think that's the Sinclair clan chief, from Scotland. He's this year's guest of honor."

I looked at the adoring Sinclairs in the stands surrounding their chief. "That chief's ancestors probably evicted some of the North Carolina Sinclairs' ancestors so he'd have land enough to graze sheep. And now they're all the best of friends!"

"Yes." Grandma D. smiled, not hearing—or perhaps overlooking—the sarcasm in my voice. "Isn't that wonderful?"

I studied my knees. The idea probably deserved some thought. And I might have *given* the idea that thought if some kid down the row hadn't shouted, "There they are!"

I looked off to the right. Hundreds—maybe thousands—of bagpipers were assembling beyond the field. I saw sun glinting on drums, and a million pipes sticking in the air. What had I been thinking? One pipe made a noise resembling a cat in heat. Miguel's band that morning—eight screaming cats—had set my teeth on edge. How was I going to get through this?

But when everyone else stood up, I did, too. The man beside me sloshed soda on my shoe and didn't even notice. We all watched the milling pipers gradually form straight lines. Lots of lines, wide as a football field, flanked by the drummers. The drum majors, or whatever they're called, darted about like miniature commandants.

Gradually the chatter in the stands died. An unnatural, expectant hush settled over the afternoon. The musicians stood frozen now, too, waiting.

Waiting.

Waiting.

I was about to start shrieking when a faint shout drifted through the silence. With military precision, a hundred drums began to rattle. I felt as much as heard them. The bleachers trembled beneath my feet. The very marrow of my bones, the cells and molecules and genes, started to quiver.

Then the first rank of pipers marched onto the field, and the drones of two hundred bagpipes began to wail. The wall of sound hit with staggering force. My camcorder slid from sweat-slick fingers onto the bleacher seat. I could no more steady a video camera through this than I could fly away.

The sound only grew as the lines drew closer. The melody burst from two hundred chanters. "Scotland the Brave."

That quivering in my cells intensified. A lump rose in my throat. My vision blurred, and I existed alone in a vacuum with this shuddering, gut-wrenching, soul-stirring wave of noise.

Someone reached for my hand, pressed something into my fingers. A tissue. I wiped my eyes and blearily saw Grandma D. smiling at me.

Down below, the first row of pipers passed us. When they reached the far end of the field, they turned back, mingling smartly with the ranks of pipers coming along behind. I snuffled and wiped my eyes again and again, mesmerized by the kaleidoscope of color and sound.

It took the bands three passes of the field to finish the song. The people in the stands erupted into a frenzy of approval. My knees gave way. I sank to the bleacher seat.

Grandma Dokken sat down, too, holding out the little packet of tissues. "Here," she shouted over the din. "I think you need the rest."

"Y-you don't understand," I wept, accepting the packet. "I n-never cry."

She nodded knowingly. "Don't mind, dear. That one always gets me, too, right here." She tapped her chest.

I blew my nose and wiped my eyes and tried to regain a modicum of composure. But then the massed bands started up again. "Amazing Grace," this time. I got pulled to my feet by an invisible force, and the faucets opened up all over again.

I—the MacDonald princess who had never given a rat's fanny about anything Scottish—managed to stay on my feet for the rest of my first massed band concert. But I couldn't stop crying.

Chapter 20

When it was all over, the crowd bubbled from the bleachers like lava. I sat. Grandma D. didn't seem to mind. She sat, too.

The bands had marched from the field, but some of the pipers straggled back to meet kith and kin. I saw Miguel walking along with bagpipes over his shoulder, scanning the stands. When he saw us, he bounded up to our perch. He gave his grandmother a peck on the cheek and asked me, "So, what did you think?"

"It was something else," I admitted.

"Did you get it all on tape?"

"Well . . . um . . . no."

His shoulders sagged. "You *said*," he began to complain, then went silent. I'd stopped crying, but my eyes felt damp and puffy. A miniature mountain of wadded-up tissues had grown on my lap. I watched Miguel's gaze take in the telltale detritus. His eyebrows raised, and he looked at me again.

"It was marvelous," Grandma Dokken declared. "As always."

I wasn't ready to talk about—about whatever had just happened. "Are you done?" I asked Miguel. "My mom said she'd like to meet you both, if you've got the time."

Miguel was still looking at me, eyes narrowed speculatively, but he didn't push it. "Yes, I'm done." He sounded like he wasn't sure if this was cause for celebration or not. Grandma D. said she was free until five o'clock, when she'd promised to help dismantle the Armstrong booth.

We swam upstream through the throngs to the Glen O' the Clans. The Gordons—they of the fabricated castle—were celebrating their Best Clan Tent award. "The Gordon motto is 'Remaining,'" a good-looking guy with waist-length hair and a fur cape proclaimed, toasting the Gordon pack. "We built to remain."

"There will be no joy in MacDonaldville," I muttered over my shoulder. But as we approached the MacDonald tent, I stopped so abruptly that Miguel stepped on my heel.

"Hey, watch it," he protested.

I would have fled if they hadn't been with me. The afternoon was already brimming with melodrama. Now my cup runneth over. "That's my mom," I muttered, pointing to the right of the tent. "And that guy she's talking to? That's my dad."

They saw us and broke off their conversation. My mother's cheeks were bright red. I couldn't help wondering if they were talking about old wounds, or about me.

I made the introductions, and Mom thanked Grandma Dokken for having me to supper the night before. "Oh, it was our pleasure!" the older woman insisted. Somehow, with a rare dollop of luck, the fact that I'd invited myself escaped mention.

Miguel greeted Mom warmly, then extended his hand to my father. "How do you do, sir?" he asked, his tone cooler than before. I felt absurdly grateful for that.

After a few moments of polite small talk, my friends excused themselves, and I was left alone with my parents. Blessedly, Nan appeared before the silence descended from awkward to painful. "C'mon, Daddy," she cried. "You promised me ice cream before the awards ceremony!"

Dad looked at me. "Want to come, Tanya?"

I was done. Exhausted. Empty. "No thanks."

Dad twisted his mouth unhappily, but Nan had already turned away. I watched them disappear through the grove. Mom's hand landed on my shoulder. "Are you O.K.?"

"Sure!" I tried. But Mom didn't fall off the proverbial potato truck—or tattie truck, in Scots parlance—yesterday. I knew that *she* knew I'd been crying.

"Tanya . . ." She hesitated. "I wanted this to be something we could share. You and me and Nanag. But I know you haven't had much fun this weekend—"

"Mary!" It was that Doug fellow. He stood at the front

table with two visitors, a young couple. "Do we have any more prints of Armadale Castle?"

"I put inventory lists on—the—*boxes!*" I said, frustration leaking through.

Mom gave my shoulder an understanding squeeze. "There should be a few more in that carton. No, the other one, underneath the membership forms. . . ."

I watched Mom report back for MacDonald duty. She found the missing prints and explained to the visitors that yes indeed, if they became members of the Clan MacDonald organization here and now, they'd receive the print as a gift in *addition* to four newsletters a year and an annual banquet.

"Plus lots of volunteer opportunities!" Doug added. The couple took advantage of the plaid-light special and walked away clutching their prize. "Two more victims ensnared!" Doug declared dramatically when they were out of earshot.

Mom laughed with real pleasure. Then she reached up and plucked an invisible bit of lint from Doug's jacket.

Oh. *Ohhh.*

So. Maybe, just maybe, Mom wasn't still *quite* as torn up about Dad as I had thought.

Doug grinned down at Mom before turning away to greet someone else. Mom looked after him with a tiny smile, then noticed me staring. "What?" she asked.

"I, um . . . nothing. That is . . ." I shrugged and stepped closer. "Are you and Doug, you know, going to go out?"

Two new spots of color bloomed on Mom's cheeks, but her voice was calm. "Would it bother you if I went out with Doug?"

"Me? No! I just was, you know, surprised, that's all," I stammered like an idiot. "I thought you were still real upset about what Dad did." My cheeks were probably redder than Mom's.

"Well . . ." Mom tipped her head to one side. "That happened well over a year ago."

"But the divorce hasn't been final all that long. I just thought—"

"I certainly haven't forgotten what happened. I will always regret that my marriage to your father failed." She paused, considering. "But I'm not going to wear a martyr's crown for the rest of my life. I think it's time to move on, don't you?"

Who was this woman, and what had she done with my mom? "Sure!" I said brightly.

My mother put both hands on my shoulders. "Your father did a terrible thing," she said quietly, with an intent look that said, *I do know that you understand what happened.* "But I can't feed on my anger about that forever."

"You have a right to be angry," I said.

She shook her head. "I made some mistakes, too,

Tanya. I think my marriage was in trouble for years before anything happened, and I didn't do a damn thing about it."

I heard my dad: *You don't know everything you think you know.* I was starting to think I didn't know diddly about squat.

"I could spend every waking moment wondering about what might have been," Mom added, "but I choose not to. So here we are. I have the rest of my life ahead of me, and I don't intend to waste a single day."

The group at the tent burst into laughter about something. Mom's friends, having a good time. "I'm glad," I said quietly. "I really am glad about that, Mom."

"Thank you."

"Listen, I, um, want to grab a few more shots while the light is good. Catch you later, O.K.?" Mom nodded.

I headed like a lemming out through the parking field. Some of the day visitors were leaving, and the parking volunteers had evidently abandoned the scene, so things were chaotic. I sighed with relief when I safely reached the banks of Pond Scum Pond. Stopping short of throwing myself over the edge, I flopped back in the grass so I could watch the clouds.

I was a dork. A blind, self-absorbed dork.

I was happy for Mom. Truly. *Really.* She'd gone looking for roots and had maybe found something else good, too. Still, it was strange to think about her going on a date.

And there was the trouble between me and Dad hanging over my head like a broadsword.

And . . . there was this business of genetic memory to deal with. Miguel thought it was all cooler than cool. I thought it was twisted. What came next, locking myself into my bedroom with candles and a Ouija board?

But *something* had happened. Not even just that Campbell business, either. Something had seized me during that massed pipe band concert. Something had reached down deep inside and grabbed me by the gut. Thank God for Grandma Dokken, who'd sat calmly during my meltdown, handing me tissues.

I sat back up, remembering that Scottish laird sitting in front of us. How had he felt during the concert? I wondered. And I remembered my snotty comment about his ancestors evicting tenants during the Clearances. He, and the descendants of those poor evicted souls, seemed to have moved on.

Just like Dad had. And Nan, and even Mom. The only one who hadn't was me.

For a while I stared at the duckweed covering the pond, all those tiny, indistinguishable flowering plants contributing their own wee bit of life to the universe.

Then I got up and walked back through the near-gridlock of exiting cars to the festival grounds, and on to the dance arena. A couple of kilted officials were dragging a podium to one corner of the stage, and a third was arranging medals and trophies on a table behind it. The dance competitions had concluded; the only thing left was the exhibition dances and presentation of awards.

Weekend-weary dance parents trickled toward the benches for the last hurrah, and day visitors trudged toward the parking lot. I did a quick scan, but Dad and Nan were evidently still finishing off the promised ice cream. So I waited, pacing, anxious now to get on with it. Soon I saw them walking toward me, Nan's face tilted toward Dad with an eager smile.

I strode over to meet them. "Hi," I announced. "Dad, we need to talk."

"I'm dancing in the exhibition reel!" Nan wailed. "It's almost time!"

Dad looked from one daughter to the other. "Can this wait until—"

"No, it really can't wait." I'd finally figured out what I needed to say. I couldn't let the moment go by.

Dad kissed Nan on the top of her head. "You go and find Miss Janet, Kitten. I'll be along in a minute." He waited until she had gone before turning back to me. I could tell by the tightening of his mouth that he was annoyed. "Tanya, I have tried repeatedly to talk with you this weekend. What is so urgent now?"

"It's about—well, the thing is . . ." I took a deep breath. Why was it so hard to just tell him how I felt? I tried to conjure up the words I'd formed so firmly in my head back by the pond and instead wondered insanely if the acting lessons he kept trying to foist on me would give me the self-confidence to confront *him*. That was probably not what he had in mind when offering his checkbook.

"Tanya, I am waiting!" He glanced toward the stage area. "And so is your sister."

"I *know!*" I tried again. "The thing is—"

"Jim?" someone said. "That's it, isn't it? Jim . . . Jim Zeshonski!"

Standing at my elbow was none other than Christina's father. I had truly entered *The Twilight Zone*.

My dad met the man's handshake, groping for a name as recognition sank in. "Andy Campbell! From the NCSS conference in San Antonio!"

I stood like a mannequin while they reminisced. My dad, the geography teacher, had attended the National Council for the Social Studies conference the same year Mr. Campbell, who worked for a map company, made a presentation about computerized imaging. They'd chatted after the workshop and ended up having Margaritas and Mexican food on the River Walk. It all sounded very cozy.

Christina's father scratched the bridge of his nose. "What was that, two years ago?"

"Must have been three!" Dad insisted. "What the heck are you doing here? Do you live nearby?"

"Not too far," Mr. Campbell said. "My daughter's big

on this competitive Highland dancing." He shrugged, as if trying to convey that this was no big deal, but his pride shone like a sunrise. "She's got more trophies than Tiger Woods. Got her first one when she was about eight, can you believe it? I don't know where she got the talent— not from me, that's for sure. All that time dancing, and she still makes honor roll, every term. Wants to go to law school one day." He glanced at me and cleared his throat. "Anyway, how about you? Didn't you live up north some- place?"

"Still do—Wisconsin," Dad said. "I'm down visiting my daughters. This is Tanya."

He gestured toward me. And I waited for him to say something more. I willed him to say something, *any- thing,* more.

"Look, it's good to see you," Dad said. "But I gotta run. My younger daughter's doing an exhibition dance."

My blood began to simmer in my veins.

"Of course—Nanag!" Mr. Campbell smacked his forehead. "We've met." He didn't mention that he'd met me, too.

Dad turned toward the arena as the microphone squawked in warning. "I need to get down there."

"I hear that," Mr. Campbell said, and they shook hands again.

"We really need to grab seats," Dad said to me when Christina's father had gone ahead. "We'll talk later, O.K.?"

I couldn't even answer. Every muscle was rigid. This had nothing to do with ancestral memory, or my mother, or the stress of moving to North Carolina. This had everything to do with me and my father the geography-teacher-turned-thespian.

He didn't even wait for an answer. I followed him down to the benches and watched him take a seat. He obviously expected me to sit beside him.

I kept walking.

A few small groups of dancers clustered to one side of the stage—those selected to demonstrate each dance before the final trophies were awarded. I saw Nan waiting near Miss Janet. On stage four girls were hopping through the *Seann Triubhas* while one of the judges provided enlightened commentary for the spectators—most of whom were dancers just waiting to hear the winners announced.

I presented myself in front of my dance teacher, who was trying to wipe a chocolate stain from a little girl's vest with a shredding tissue. "Miss Janet."

"As you can see, the dancers remain on the balls of their feet," the announcer droned. She sounded tired. "This is one of the most challenging aspects of Highland dancing."

"Miss Janet!" I hissed. "I want to do the sword dance."

That got her attention. "You . . . *what?*" she managed. Nan stared.

"I want to do the sword dance!"

The piper droned to a halt. The panting dancers took

their bows and pranced from the stage. "And now the winner of the seventeen-and-under Premier class, *Seann Triubhas,*" the announcer said. She fumbled with a piece of paper. "Christina Campbell of the Misty Glen School of Highland Dance!"

The crowd broke into applause—polite congratulations from the general spectators, wild hoots of approval from Christina's fan club. Nan forgot to gape at me and burst into enthusiastic applause. I watched from the wings as Christina came forward to accept her medal, managing to look pleased and surprised and graceful and humble, all at once.

Did I hate her because of some centuries-old feud? Or because she was such a good dancer, and a better role model for Nan than me?

Christina bowed prettily to the crowd. I heard her dad bellow, "Go, Christina!"

Or did I hate Christina because her dad just about peed himself with pride every time she walked by?

"Next we have the sword dance," the announcer crackled. "Our exhibition dancers are from the Purple Heather School of Highland Dancing. . . ."

"I'm doing this," I announced to Miss Janet. She stammered something inaudible. I marched up the steps.

I remember positioning myself on the stage between two other girls who no doubt wondered what the heck was going on, and watching the official place the crossed swords on the stage in front of me. I remember spotting my dad in the sparse crowd. I remember hearing the piper begin *"Gillie Chalium."*

Then I dug down deep, really deep, and I don't remember much else. Music. Mist. The scent of something damp and earthy. An exultant fire in the blood.

And then it was all over. I was back on that flimsy stage at the Cross Creek Highland Games. I turned to march primly away. Instead of falling in line, the other two dancers, wide-eyed, scuttled backwards to let me pass. As I went down the steps, Nan and Miss Janet stared as if they'd never seen me before.

"Thank you," I said politely to my dance teacher. My blood had subsided to a pleasant tingle. I felt marvelous.

Her mouth opened and closed a few times. "Where," she finally managed, "did you learn to do *that?*"

I smiled and shrugged and went to find my father. I sat beside him in silence, not meeting his astonished gaze, until Nan's exhibition performance was done. Then I faced him. "I want to talk, Dad," I said in a firm whisper. "Now."

I marched up the aisle, trusting he would follow. As soon as we were out of earshot of the last-row benches, I stopped. "Here's the thing, Dad," I began. "It doesn't seem to bother you that Nan and I moved a thousand miles away."

"What?" He blinked.

I stared at a family heading toward the parking lot. A little girl in pink leggings skipped in front, clutching a balloon. But I didn't see that little girl. I saw me: Happy behind the camera, or editing footage on my old computer. Vegetarian. Supreme organizer. Tanya MacDonald Zeshonski, average kid. "It wasn't just Mom," I insisted finally. "Nan and I got dumped, too."

"That is *not* true."

"Oh yeah? Well, you know what? It feels like it. And here's the other thing, Dad. I know you're proud of Nan, but have you ever been proud of me? Even for a minute?"

"Proud? Well—I—of course I'm proud of you."

"What for?" I demanded. "Tell me one thing you're proud of."

His mouth moved like a beached herring's. "Tanya, this is ridiculous," he managed. "I'm your father, and—"

"I know you're my father! But I'm not a little kid anymore, so don't talk to me like one. All you've ever done is try to change me into someone else. I don't want to be an actress, Dad. I don't want to be a competitive dancer. I want to make documentaries. Why can't you just accept me the way I am? Do you even *like* me?"

"I was just trying to be helpful when I suggested acting lessons!" Dad's face was turning red again. "And it's not like you've ever gone out of your way to be supportive of my interests."

I felt as if I'd been slapped. "That's not true! I went to

some of your plays. And I always was around for your school stuff—"

"Have you ever been proud of *me,* Tanya?" Dad asked, his voice low and hard. "Do you even like *me?*"

"I—what are you talking about?" I sputtered. "How about the time I cleaned up your office? And—"

"And I couldn't find anything for a month afterwards," he muttered.

"*What?*" I remembered my heroic efforts to make order from chaos, armed with colored file folders and computer-printed labels. "Well, excuse me for bothering. I was just trying to be helpful." We stood glaring at each other, panting as if we'd been in a boxing match.

"I've spent twenty-one years teaching geography," he growled. "Half of my students don't care if the world is flat or round. Most don't understand why cultural geography even matters in our global society. No one's ever said, 'Thanks, Mr. Zeshonski. Good job.'" He ran a hand through his hair. "You grew up watching me work on lesson plans, and search out the best maps and tools, and spend evening after evening trying to find new ways to get kids excited about a subject I care passionately for. And I don't remember you ever saying, 'Wow, Dad. Way to go. I'm proud of you.'"

I folded my arms over my chest. He wasn't playing the part I'd expected when I'd rehearsed this scene in my head.

"Sometimes," Dad said more quietly, "I think you and I are too much alike."

Alike? We were nothing alike. Were we? Besides, he was the parent here. When daughters finally found the words to talk about hurt feelings, dads weren't supposed to talk about their own. Were they?

Dad closed his eyes, his mouth twisting sideways. Finally he looked at me again. "Tanya, we're getting off track here. I need you to understand something. Your mother and I didn't get a divorce because of one momentary lapse in judgment on my part. It had been coming for a long time."

That's not true, I wanted to yell. We were a happy family before you ruined everything!

But I remembered Mom telling me she'd made mistakes, too. I thought of all those evenings, Dad in his study working on school stuff, Mom at the library doing genealogy stuff, Nan off at Girl Scouts or gymnastics, me doing homework. . . . Maybe we had all been going in different directions for a long time. Maybe I'd created the memory that suited me, just as some people choose what aspects of Scottish heritage they want to celebrate.

"Your mother and I had problems," Dad went on. "We grew apart. I made mistakes. I'll take the rap for that. But none of it had anything to do with you. Got it?"

I wasn't sure. It had taken me this long to figure out exactly why I was so angry at my dad. I couldn't just make a left turn now and leave it all behind. Instead I rubbed my shoulders. Shrugged once. Nodded.

Dad looked at me, away, finally back at me. "I'd like to spend some time with you this summer," he said. "You're always welcome at my new house. Or we could go away. Maybe take a trip up north. To Lake Superior. Maybe to the Apostle Islands? You could bring a friend if you wanted. Maybe you could come in time for my new musical, and then we could go—"

"Yeah, O.K., Dad." I was drowning in his flood of words. "I'll think about it."

"Good. Good."

"You should go back down there before Nan goes ballistic."

He nodded again. "See you later?"

"Sure. Well . . . wait. I'll come with you."

He nodded, and we filed silently back down the aisle. I wasn't ready to figure out the next step. I'd had a truly honest conversation with my father, maybe for the first time ever. Honest both ways. I needed some time to sort out what had been said.

But something was different. The almost-stroke feeling was gone. What I had right then was worth savoring.

Chapter 21

Mom gave Nan permission to go out to dinner with Dad, but I politely declined his invitation to join them. We'd made enough progress for one day.

I looked at my watch as they headed out to join the crawling line of exiting vehicles. Quarter to five. Mom would be at least another hour, maybe more, helping dismantle the clan tent. I headed for the campground. I swung by Miguel's site to say good-bye, but no one was there.

Mom had left our campsite in fairly good shape, but I did take down the tent and wrestle that into the car. I'd just started considering what else I could do to get this show on the road when a shrill wail made me jump. I turned around and saw Miguel grinning, fingering his pipes.

"You," I said, "are an evil person."

"Yeah." He'd changed into jeans and a sweatshirt and had a paper bag under his arm. "You got a few minutes?"

I snorted. "You gotta be kidding. Mom'll be the last MacDonald out of here."

"Then come on. I want to show you something."

"What?" I stared pointedly at the bagpipes.

"Just come *on*." He grabbed my hand and tugged me out of the campsite.

"You can be a real pain in the ass sometimes," I observed.

"Yeah. You too." But he didn't let go of my hand.

The visitors were almost gone now. We walked through the grounds—past vendors in vans and trailers inching toward their tents and the monumental job of packing up.

Suddenly I spotted Christina Campbell and her father walking just ahead of us. Several medals hung from ribbons around her neck. She'd evidently once again accumulated the highest number of points in the Premier class, because her father carried a huge trophy. I stopped.

"What?" Miguel asked, then followed my gaze. "Is that her?"

"That's her."

"She doesn't look too evil."

I hesitated. Should I approach her? Try to make amends, to bury the broadsword? *Well, Christina, Mr. Campbell, your people did my people some serious wrong. But hey, that was centuries ago, and my people were no saints either, so maybe it's time to move on.*

"You want to talk to her?" Miguel asked. "I'll wait."

"Not today." I sighed. I *would* talk with Christina . . . as soon as I figured out what to say.

Miguel shot me a sidelong look as we started walking again. "What?" I demanded.

"I've been debating whether to tell you something."

"Tell me *what*?"

"Ever since you told me about your thing with Christina Campbell, I've been trying to remember why that rang a bell. I finally remembered. There's some story about a piper who was either a MacDonald or loyal to the MacDonalds. He got imprisoned by the Campbells, and he played his bagpipes to warn his MacDonald chieftain of a planned ambush. The chieftain heard the warning and escaped. But the Campbells were so pissed that they chopped off the piper's hands—"

"Eee-ooo," I protested.

"And he bled to death. And now his ghost haunts the castle and the moors, still playing his pipes."

"Nice folks, those Campbells."

"The point is," he looked at me triumphantly, "maybe you shouldn't be so hard on pipers, eh?"

"I never meant to be hard on pipers, just on pipes themselves."

Miguel laughed and led me on past the athletic fields, past the merchants, past even the farthest row of porta-johns. We finally stopped at a little meadow, bordered by the omnipresent loblolly pines.

"You want to sit?" Miguel asked. He laid his bagpipes carefully on the grass.

"O.K." I wasn't sure why we were here, but I didn't see any point in arguing.

He held out the paper bag. "I got you a present."

"Um . . . thanks." I felt flustered, like a fifth grader who gets an unexpected valentine. I opened the bag and found a T-shirt bearing a lovely silk-screened version of the Scottish emblem. And underneath, the words "Kiss My Thistle." I couldn't help smiling.

"It made me think of you."

"You shouldn't have."

"I got it cheap. End-of-weekend discount." He picked up a dead pine needle, snapped it in two, tossed the pieces aside. "So . . . what went on during the concert?"

"The massed bands?" I stretched out my legs slowly and regarded my toes. "Honest to God, Miguel, I don't know."

"But you felt something, didn't you." It wasn't a question.

"I did." I drew a deep, long breath, then slowly exhaled. "And there's more."

"Yeah?"

"Yeah." It took a few more deep breaths, but I told Miguel what I could about my performance at the sword dance earlier. "I hardly even remember it. Nan told me it was 'like a regular sword dance—only different. Kind of fiery. Sort of.'" Nan had still been stammering when the awards ceremony was complete, unable to find the right words. "And she told me that Miss Janet said she'd never seen anyone dance with such abandon." I looked at him.

"In a way, it still creeps me out," I said. "But in another way, it was kinda cool. I didn't get cold or feel like I was about to puke."

"That is so unbelievable!" Envy was splashed all over Miguel's face.

"And right after that, I talked to my dad. Not just about him and Mom. About him and me."

"Yeah?"

"I don't really like my dad," I said slowly. "And I'm not sure he really likes me." I nibbled my lower lip. "He said we're a lot alike in some ways. It pissed me off when he said that. But maybe it is a little bit true."

Miguel was wise enough to hold his tongue.

"The thing is . . . I think he used to be a better dad before everything happened," I said. "And I was happier then. But he's happier now." I shrugged, going for nonchalant. "Anyway. He's still my dad, I guess."

"The only one you've got." Miguel mulled that over in silence for a moment. "At least you talked."

"Yeah." I picked some dirt from beneath my fingernail. "My dad wants to spend time with me this summer." I hesitated and switched to shredding a blade of grass. "You want to see Lake Superior sometime?"

He sat up straight. "No kidding?"

"Well, maybe we could go. I'm not ready to spend a week with him by myself. I'm sure he'd spring for two plane tickets. He said I could bring a friend."

Miguel nodded, staring ahead. I imagined him contemplating the possibilities that Lake Superior offered an aquatic botanist. Shadows were starting to stretch across the meadow, and I wondered how Mom was coming at the clan tent, but I wasn't ready to head back yet.

Then Miguel looked at me. "So," he said. "Are you going to do anything about what's been happening?"

"With my dad?"

"No. The other stuff."

I shot him a glance. "Do? What am I supposed to do?"

"Well . . . I don't know exactly. But, Tanya, you've opened up some kind of channel this weekend, don't you think?"

"No. I don't know. Maybe."

"All I'm saying is, you might be able to take it further. Maybe you could even learn more about your own ancestors. Wouldn't that be cool?"

"My mom's already done our genealogy—"

"I don't mean names and dates. I mean find the real people. Learn their stories."

"I don't know that I even want to do that," I protested, but suddenly I wondered again if I was descended from one of those anonymous kick-ass women I'd read about. "And even if I did . . . I wouldn't know where to begin!"

"I could help you."

"Oh yeah?"

"I've done a lot of reading," he informed me loftily. "Where did you say you lived? Laurinburg?"

"Outside Laurinburg. Northeast."

"Well, that's not so far from Fayetteville. Maybe we can get together and talk more about it."

"O.K. Maybe. But listen, I want to work on a new documentary first." Shrugging off the willies, I told him about my plan. I told him I was going to make a documentary about Scottish women. Not ancient, long-dead ones. But real women who, for reasons still not entirely clear to me, found some kind of strength in affiliating with this whole Scottish thing.

Women like my mother, whose world fell apart but chose not to spend her days sitting in a lavender bathrobe watching television, and instead created a whole new life for herself.

Women like Grandma Dokken, who'd survived the Korean War and lost two husbands, and had her only daughter move to Puerto Rico, and still took delight in green M&M's and Scottish country dancing.

Women like Sheila Silber, Goddess of Heavy Sports, who turned the male tartan establishment on its ear with good humor and deeds done, not whining.

"I suppose . . . maybe . . . even women like Christina Campbell," I said grudgingly. "I'm not sure about that part, though."

He shook his head approvingly. "Either way, the whole thing could be excellent."

"I think so, too."

For a moment we sat in silence. Miguel sat with his head cocked, as if listening for something, although I couldn't imagine what. A hawk circled lazily over the meadow, then moved on. A car honked somewhere in the distance behind us.

"So," I said, gesturing toward the bagpipes. "You didn't bring me out here for a private concert, did—"

"Sh!" Miguel held up one hand.

I waited until my patience ran out—maybe ten seconds. "What are you listening to?"

"Do you hear any bagpiping? Real faint?"

I strained my ears, then grinned. "No. For the first time in almost three days, I do not."

He looked disappointed. "For a moment I thought I did. There was this famous North Carolina piper once, Alexander MacRae. He died—oh, almost a century ago, I guess. They say that sometimes, when a Highland Games is winding down and almost everybody has gone, you can still hear old Alexander playing his pipes. He favors meadows, they say."

I rolled my eyes. "I suspect all anybody ever hears is the echo of the massed bands ringing in their heads. It's probably a medical phenomenon. Bagpipe-head."

We sat for a while longer. Miguel was still listening for the phantom piper. Me, I was just content. Finally Miguel sighed. "I suppose we should—"

I jerked erect and grabbed his arm. Faintly, almost imperceptibly, I heard bagpipe music. It echoed across the meadow, soft and poignant. Then it faded away.

For a moment we both sat rigid, straining to hear, but nothing more came. I looked at Miguel. "Did you hear that?"

He grinned. "Yeah! That was unbelievable!"

"It was probably just some piper giving a last tootle before heading home," I said, but you know what? I didn't believe it. I didn't even want to believe it.

Miguel didn't believe it, either. "I'm going to play for old man MacRae." He stood up, positioned his instrument, and began. He chose a strathspey, cheerful and full of life.

I bobbed my toes in time. Finally, the tune pulled me to my feet. I kicked off my Birkies and moved behind Miguel, where no one but Alexander MacRae could see me.

I didn't have a targe to dance on. I didn't care. While Miguel played his bagpipes, I danced a Highland fling.

$\mathcal{A}$cknowledgments

I'm grateful to the many people who helped this project take shape. Clan McStraw showed me what true Scottish hospitality is all about at the 2004 Grandfather Mountain Highland Games. Members of the Heather Highland Dancers and Madison Pipes and Drums, of Madison, Wisconsin, allowed me to visit their practice sessions. Susan Jeffrey-Borger and Adam Borger patiently answered many questions about dancing and piping. Although most of the books mentioned in the novel are fictional, I found *Damn' Rebel Bitches: The Women of the '45* by Maggie Craig (Edinburgh and London: Mainstream Publishing, 1997) helpful for gaining insight into Scottish women's roles during that turbulent period.

Claire-Michelle Young, Kay Klubertanz, Tom Micksch, and other friends from my WPT days (you know who you are) taught me what little I know about making television. Cynthia Nolen provided that opportunity in the first place.

Warm thanks also to Eileen Daily, Marsha Dunlap, Amy Laundrie, Katie Mead, and Gayle Rosengren for their friendship and insights; to my agent, Andrea Cascardi, for her help along the way; and to Debby Vetter, Ron McCutchan, and the rest of the Cricket Books team, for all their care. And to Scott—thanks for putting on the kilt.